River Road Stories

Mary Eschbach

Illustrations by
P. G. Williams

For Tony,
Who qualifies to be a
genuine skeeter beater!

Mary Eschbach

River Road Stories
by Mary Eschbach

Illustrations by
P. G. Williams

Copyright 2007

Published by Chapin House Books (2007)

ISBN 10: 0-9771079-8-1
ISBN 13: 978-0-9771079-8-8

Chapin House Books
A division of
The Florida Historical Society Press
435 Brevard Avenue
Cocoa, FL 32922
www.fhspress.org

Dedication

For my Mom, who gave me a love of nature

For my Dad, who gave me a love of art and literature

For my dogs, who waited patiently

For all 'skeeter beaters, that their stories
will not be forgotten

Acknowledgements

Thanks to: Mom and Dad for their stories and encouragement, L.A. Davis for proofreading and lots of moral support, Mr. and Mrs. E. for proofreading and corrections, Ms. Williams for the beautiful illustrations, Goot and Goldie for all the good advice and help with this project, Mr. Pat Smith for his kind words and thoughts, Troy for quiet office space, and Tammy for invaluable I-T support.

M. E.

TABLE OF CONTENTS

1—Ruby Red

She was the girl next door, as ineffable yet as familiar as the river that shaped our lives. I lived beside her as my grandparents had lived next door to hers many years before, a continuity as surely felt as the presence of the river, a common thread running though our lives, binding us all together, one generation to the next. We lived on the beautiful Indian River, famous for its citrus fruit, abundant wildlife, exotic tropical flora and fauna, and great fishing and hunting, but to me, it was special because Red was my neighbor and best pal. She was older than I by several years, but she always let me tag along on her many adventures. And although she never had red hair, we called her "Red," short for Ruby Red—her given name.

As it happened, she was named for a variety of beautiful red grapefruit. Her father was a local citrus baron, admittedly eccentric, as was her whole family, and named his children for his favorite types of citrus fruit. Her brother was named Duncan Temple, for the best varieties of grapefruit and oranges, respectively. Red never complained about her unusual name, but always said, with her typical droll humor, "I'm just thankful my father's favorite orange isn't the navel."

Of course, their unusual names inevitably led to comments about her "fruity" family, but these never seemed to faze her—she was the first to admit that she came from a long line of eccentrics, and she was resigned to that dubious inheritance.

We grew up in a relatively calm world—after the horror of WWII and before the Viet Nam debacle. It was a time of great optimism and seemingly endless possibilities.

We lived in a magical place—the River Road was a little piece of paradise on the coquina-lined banks of the historic Indian River. Everyone had an orange grove behind his home, and in the spring, the air was perfumed with the heady fragrance of orange blossoms.

As a rule, we got up early in the morning, for we always had many things to do, places to explore, and not a moment to waste. After feeding all the critters, we usually started out eating a few sweet oranges, whatever variety was ripest at the time, and seeing what was happening in the groves and perhaps engaging in rotten-orange warfare. As in all warfare, there were strict rules, but only two: picking oranges was strictly *verboten*, as Red's family sold them; and only well-ripened oranges could be used—unripe oranges hurt too much if they hit their mark. Besides, the really rotten fruit made much more desirable ammo, as they splattered all over, making a big, gooey mess when they hit someone.

After playing in the grove, we would head for the river, rock-hopping along the coquina, looking for interesting things at the water's edge. One never knew what one would find—maybe a fiddler crab or an interesting piece of flotsam or jetsam.

"Is this flotsam or jetsam?" Red would ask, smiling slyly: She knew there was a difference, albeit not a great one, but made me look it up in the dictionary. We always had our best days beachcombing after a big storm or hurricane, sometimes even finding water skiis, fishing "bobbers," boat cushions, or various kinds of lumber, real treasures to us. Duncan and Red often lashed together the lumber to make a raft, which they would pole up and down the river, *a la* Huck Finn.

Sometimes we would find a fish skeleton, or one of those curious, prehistoric creatures called the horseshoe crab. These interesting marine arthropods with many legs and a sharp tail were plentiful and would wash up on the shore. In the shallow water around the spoil islands they could be seen gliding along the sandy bottom, their horseshoe-shaped hard carapace, or shell, protecting them from most predators. Unlike the stingaree, which also cruised these waters, they were harmless.

It was because of the stingarees that we usually wore old tennis shoes in the river. Our "river shoes" were the ones that had been worn out by countless miles of running and biking, the river shoe designation being the last gasp in the life of a tennis shoe—the next stage would be the garbage. Red's brother, Duncan, was famous for making his shoes last longer than anyone else's—he did this with the magic of adhesive tape. Sometimes his mom would find him using a whole roll of tape on his shoes, going round and round the toe, holding the shoes together a while longer, delaying their inevitable, ignominious demise in the garbage can. One can only wonder how long he could have kept them going with the modern-day duct tape.

We investigated everything, with dogs at our sides, and I received a great education in natural history, biology, and life, at Red's hands.

She taught me how the pelicans were able to glide just over the water surface without beating their wings, how fiddler crabs got their name, and how the perfectly round holes were formed in the coquina rock. Red sure knew a lot about a lot of things. She was a voracious reader and had plenty of book learning, but she said most of her education was simply from observation.

"Shrimpette," she would say, (that was her pet name for me), "If you keep your eyes and ears open, and your mouth shut, Mother Nature will teach you most of what you need to know."

Our River Road curved tortuously amid the cabbage palms and the crooked oaks. Their great, graceful branches sometimes bent so far as to touch each other above the road, forming a tunnel of trees called an "oak alley" in these parts.

"This was once a dirt road and it used to be US 1—the only road on the East Coast of Florida," Red explained. "Long before that, of course, it was probably an Indian trail. Before the time of automobiles it was planted with the large-limbed trees to provide shade for the horses which pulled the carriages and wagons. Later, when cars first appeared, it was an exciting occurrence when one would pass, and everyone would come out on his porch to see it. Some days one or two would pass, some days, none."

In fact, in those early days of automobiles, there was no such thing as a driver's license; Red's mom started driving at age twelve. Later, when licenses were required, one could buy them at the drugstore. Red's dad got his at Lovett's Grocery Store, the forerunner of Winn-Dixie.

In the morning when the river was calm, it looked like white-hot molten gold, and in the summer, the heat radiating off it felt like a furnace. Red was often gone in the summer, as her family loved to travel; she always said she was fortunate to have traveled so much, that traveling afforded the best education one could have.

I missed her and our many adventures when she was gone, as Red was always a good companion and fun playmate to me. But most of all, I missed our daily hikes and bike rides down the River Road, exploring anything that looked interesting, discussing life, our dreams, and ambitions. When she was old enough to drive, we would take long, slow rides in her convertible. As in everything else we did, we were always accompanied by one or more of her faithful Labrador retrievers. They sat in the back seat, ears flapping, nose sniffing the wind, barking at passing dogs in yards—as if to taunt them, "I'm riding with my mistress in the convertible—aren't I the lucky dog!" I don't know who enjoyed those rides more, the dogs or us. Those drives allowed us time for long conversations, and I would listen with rapt attention to her many stories of her life, our parents' and grandparents' lives, and of the mysteries of nature and mankind as she perceived them; she was ever patient with me, for just as Chaucer's student, "Gladly would (s)he learn, and gladly teach."

We lived happily in a world in which we knew our place, and were thus secure. It was a time when parents were in control, people were responsible for their actions, and private property was respected. Elders were looked up to not only just because they were older, but also for their wisdom; no matter your age, anyone older than yourself was addressed respectfully as ma'am or sir, as Mr, Mrs, or Miss. Actually, here in the South, Mrs and Miss were generally pronounced the same, as a drawn out Miz: we were years ahead of the feminist Ms. It was a time when schools and parents still believed in discipline and in learning the 3 R's, a time when mothers imparted good manners to their children, and fathers were considered the ultimate authority in the household, a time when almost all kids had two parents in the house with the same name as theirs.

It was a time when, as Red said, men were men, women were women, and those who weren't kept it to themselves. It was a world where we didn't lock our homes or cars; it was a simple world and a time when people had values and the guts to impose them—a world thus made comfortable and safe to live in. To be sure, evil existed then, and crime, but the small towns were mostly inhabited by decent folks, and life for us as children was happy and carefree, filled with little daily discoveries and delights that seemed big to us: it didn't take much to amuse us. As the poet Robert Herrick said, "Where care none is, slight things do lightly please." No doubt everyone would return to that idyllic time if they could.

I have tried with a loving memory, but one naturally hazed by the passage of time, to set down Red's stories and thoughts with some kind of fidelity to the originals, knowing the difficulty of the task. I will leave it to the reader to interpret them, to enjoy the memories of a time lost and not to be seen again. For even now, when looking back, I wonder, "Could it have really been that way? How did our town change so much in such a short time? What would Red think of our world now? Was her life real or just a dream?"

With no tangible answers, but feeling the certainty of her absence, here begin the River Road stories as I remember them, shared with me as a growing girl on the banks of the Indian River—the philosophy of life, love, and nature, according to Red.

2—The River

In the early days of Florida settlers, the Indian River was the common thread that bound people together in these parts. In those times, the pioneers settled along its banks and the river provided them their livelihood and sustenance. It was their source of communication with the rest of Florida and the United States and was their watery lifeline in a sometimes harsh and inhospitable environment.

The Indian River is more properly termed a lagoon or estuary, as it is a brackish body of water, with freshwater streams emptying into it, and with openings to the ocean; it is separated from the Atlantic by a large sandbar, or barrier island, which holds numerous beach communities. For many miles there are actually two rivers separated by another strip of land called Merritt Island. The topography is rather confusing, but imagine traveling from the Atlantic Ocean west to Cocoa: you would first pass across the barrier island called Cocoa Beach, then over the Banana River, then across Merritt Island, then over the Indian River, then finally you would arrive at

7

Cocoa. The distance as the seagull flies is about ten miles. Today it is a drive of a half hour; fifty years ago it was an all day excursion to go to the beach by way of dirt roads and old wooden bridges.

Red's mom and her friends used to pile into the back of her dad's old Model T truck (the dog often rode on the running board) and go to their beach house, which stood in the vicinity of Bernard's Surf in Cocoa Beach now. Her dad owned several hundred feet of the beach there, and sold it for a pittance in the '40's. (He also sold the old Model T truck for ten dollars, and Red's mom cried for days.) Everyone always carried a bucket on a long rope with them to the beach, for it was probable that one of the bridges would be on fire, coming or going. The bridges, being wooden, were particularly vulnerable to cigarettes, and often caught fire this way. Sometimes Red's mom and other people would get stuck at the beach or on Merritt Island if one of the bridges had burned out.

Getting to the beach was by a very circuitous route. First, you crossed the Indian River on a narrow wooden bridge from Cocoa. On this drawbridge, there was a little house where the bridge tender lived. Not only did he open the bridge for boats, but he also collected a toll. Some people paid in advance for a year and had a special tag on the front of their car. Once on Merritt Island, the road meandered north to Sykes' Creek, where you crossed the "Humpback Bridge." Then the road headed south several miles on what is now Newfound Harbor Drive to Angel City. This was the narrowest place on the Banana River, so a bridge was built there to Cocoa Beach, connecting with what is now Minuteman Causeway. Those old wooden bridges are now all gone.

Back in the days of the first white settlers, the area was a veritable paradise for sportsmen. The trade-off was the heat and the teeming hordes of mosquitoes. Driving down the road one winter day, Red observed a few ducks on the river—probably bluebills and mergansers.

"When I was a child," she said, "huge rafts of ducks would land on the river at night, and in the morning, their numbers were so great that the noise of their flapping wings would wake me at dawn as they flew away. Now their numbers are so small you hardly notice them."

In fact, in Red's parents' day the river was so thick with winter duck residents that from shore to shore, a distance of two miles or so, you couldn't see the water for all the dark feathered bodies crammed together. They used to say that you could walk across the river on their backs. In the old days, before refrigeration, people depended on the fishing and hunting to supply themselves with fresh meat. During the depression, Red's dad often awoke before daylight and went hunting before he went to school. He was only a boy, but it was a matter of survival, as money and food were scarce.

And if the bird life was abundant, the fish variety and numbers were equally prodigious. Red was always quick to point out how clear the water was when she was a girl, and how she could always catch something from her dock. Any time of the day one could catch "blowfish," funny box-shaped fish that would puff up as a defense when caught. She brought them onto the dock to amuse her dogs, then threw them back. Once plentiful, they are very scarce now in the Indian River.

As we sat on the end of her dock one day we saw a solitary jellyfish propelling itself through the water. It was a large one, maybe twelve inches across, with a white four-leaf clover design on top of its transparent, rounded body. This was the *Aurelia,* and Red allowed as how when she was young there would be huge schools of them in the springtime. Now we felt lucky to see the one lone jellyfish propelling itself peacefully along.

When August came along, hot and humid and teeming with mosquitoes, there was one wonderful, natural curiosity that made up for all the bad stuff. When the water temperature in the river reached a very warm degree, a microscopic flagellate organism called *Gonyaulex* multiplied in great numbers, causing a bioluminescence phenomenon. Any movement in the water, by a fish or a dolphin, by a net or a stick, or just plain whitecaps when the wind was whipping, would cause a bright green light in the water. This could only be seen at night, of course, and on full moon nights in August and September all the kids would be checking out the river's natural light show.

In her parents' day, fish such as speckled trout, drum, snapper, sheepshead, whiting, and redfish were the main staples of many peoples' diets. Sand sharks, sting-rays, (called stingarees by the locals), triple tail, and grouper were also plentiful, not to mention the abundant porpoise and sea cow. But that's when the river was clear as glass, and grass beds covered the sandy bottom. Shrimp, crabs, and oysters were also there in great numbers. Red's mom trapped stone crabs off their old cement dock, always snipping off just one claw and throwing the angry orange crustacean back. The claw would regrow, she would explain, and it always had one claw left with which to defend itself. Such were the laws of environmental protection in those days. There were no written rules and regulations, and there were so few people that all could share in nature's bounty without reducing it appreciably.

One time when Red's mom was a kid, an alligator had a nest of babies in a little cove by their dock. Alligators, then, as now, were infrequent visitors to our river. They prefer the freshwater St. John's River to the west.

Red's parents often had oyster roasts in their back yard. The men would go out in the river for a few hours and come back with a big No. 2 washtub brimming over with fresh, tasty oysters. Into the night they would imbibe cold beer and either steam open the succulent oysters or down them raw. The river was not polluted; its gifts were safe for consumption. When the blue crabs and shrimp were running, Red's dad would go crabbing with his buddies late at night, bringing home generous amounts for a seafood feast.

One night, after depositing the live blue crabs in the kitchen sink, he went to bed. Hours later, he awakened to a loud thump. Thinking a burglar was in the house, he crept stealthily downstairs, pistol in hand. As he walked into the kitchen, an unseen escapee blue crab on the floor grabbed his toe with its powerful pincer-claw and a terrible racket ensued. I think he would've rather faced a burglar. Times were good then, and in our childish innocence, we thought it would last forever.

But it didn't. Some people, like Red's mom, saw the changes coming before others.

"Too darn many people," she always said, and she was the first person I ever knew to foresee the coming population explosion and all the ills that have come with it. (Later on, Red would say, "You can forget all your causes, such as 'Save the Whales,' 'Save the Rain Forest,' 'Save the Manatees,' for they are all lost causes without population control—if you cannot save their habitat from destruction by humans, you cannot save the animals." She also said, "Never ever trust a so-called 'environmentalist' who has more than one or two children—he obviously doesn't get the big picture, nor is he willing to do his part to help the problem.")

The real beginning of development actually began with Henry Flagler, who built a railroad to get Northerners to his hotels which stretched from St. Augustine to Miami. Before 1850, Florida's population was only about six thousand. After Flagler, that began to mushroom, but our population here in Brevard County didn't really grow wildly until NASA appeared on the scene.

In the 1940's, the Banana River Naval Air Station, which later became Patrick Air Force Base, was built and the influx of "outsiders" began. New causeways were constructed, replacing the old wooden bridges. In the 1950's, when the US government declared its entry into the space race, and decided that Cape Canaveral was the ideal place from which to launch it, our Indian River paradise went straight to hell.

"We never knew what hit us," Red said, "We were naive babes-in-the-woods. No one was prepared for the onslaught."

There were several reasons for this, but the bottom line was the overnight influx of huge numbers of people. This is what caused all the pernicious change that was to come—and indeed, as Red so often reiterated, over-population has caused almost all the major problems our world faces today. In her parents' lifetime, she noted, the world population had tripled from less than two billion to six billion. That population explosion was felt in cities and small towns everywhere, and especially ours. In fact, since 1940, Brevard County has had a 2,800% growth in population, most of that occurring since 1960. In 1960, the population of Florida was five million. Today, forty-five years later, it is over sixteen million, with over one-half million in Brevard County.

To accommodate the new breed of "Cape workers," many things necessarily had to be "improved." Roads which were previously dirt had to be paved, picturesque drawbridges previously wooden were done away with, and large concrete causeways with high arches were put in. The Army Corps of Engineers, at the behest of the state of Florida, gladly carried out the state's plans. Salivating like Pavlov's dogs, the Corps couldn't wait to get their hands into it all: after all, they were engineers and this is what they were trained to do. And, of course, without these projects, they would have no job, so they had a vested interest in changing the face of Florida.

They contributed the system of locks connecting the Banana River to the ocean at Port Canaveral. Dredging and development of Port Canaveral began in 1950 and was completed the next year, including locks into the Banana River and a new "Barge Canal" into the Indian River. In retrospect, this has been another boondoggle, an unnecessary project made that much more insulting by the fact that the endangered manatees often get caught in the locks and are killed.

It would be years before we would see the negative results of all this "progress."

Riding around with Red in the early seventies, we noticed that Cocoa Beach was becoming a South Florida lookalike: wall-to-wall condominiums and hotels sitting on the fragile dune line, all but the very rich homeowners driven out by exorbitant property taxes. Whole swamps (now called wet-lands) where Red's dad used to hunt—most of Merritt Island—were filled in so housing developments could be built. Some of the best citrus groves in the world were taken by the government, bought at much less than their actual worth: the owners had no choice, they were told, one way or another, the space show had to go on. The river was dredged in numerous places, its shelly sand used as fill dirt. Beautiful tree-covered land was cleared at an astonishing rate to provide more land for more houses.

Of course, these changes were inevitable, given that this was Florida, but it was the *rapid* change that was so unnerving to the long-time natives.

The results of these measures of "progress" were numerous and mostly bad. Merritt Island, once the marshy hunter's paradise, would never again offer good hunting, its wildlife vastly diminished in numbers, robbed of its habitat. Causeways have caused increased silt buildup, have decreased river flow and aeration, and have increased salinity around them. This is deleterious to grass bed growth—it is estimated that the Indian River Lagoon has had a thirty percent or more loss of sea grass so far. The dredging left behind a foot-thick layer of silt, smothering grass beds and aquatic life, keeping the once clear Indian River in a perpetual state of murkiness. The increase of pavement and urban growth increased rain-water runoff into the river, carrying with it harmful pollutants, and decreasing the amount of water that goes back into the underground aquifer.

The wholesale decimation of large trees added to the heat and required that homes have air conditioning. The rise in the value of property for housing precluded replacement of citrus groves or preservation of wild lands. It is reported that there has been a seventy percent loss of scrub habitat, resulting in an eighty-seven percent loss of the beautiful, friendly, native scrub jays.

Red elaborated, "Not that citrus groves are as good a habitat as the natural vegetation, but they are sure better than sterile golf courses and housing developments." The area we lived in, Brevard County, had changed, never to be the same again. But even worse was still to come.

In the sixties and seventies the combination of rapid growth and an increasingly transient population brought heretofore unheard-of prosperity and with it, crime. For several years, Brevard was not only the fastest growing county in America, but the most drug-infested. Drugs were coming in at an alarming rate through Port Canaveral and other numerous sites on the Florida coastline. With the rapid growth, enormous amounts of money were to be made, not only in drug trafficking, but also in real estate. More boats of all kinds, shapes and sizes than one could imagine dotted the river and clogged the hundreds of marinas that seemingly sprang up overnight. Everyone was prosperous. No one cared about the land, the river, or the wildlife.

In the eighties, environmental groups began saying what Red's family and other old-timers had known all along—the Indian River estuary and surrounding land were in pitiful shape. Heavy boat traffic spelled disaster for the now endangered manatee. Original pioneers had sometimes eaten the sea cow, they were so plentiful. The prodigious duck and fish life were but a memory. Forget the once common Florida Panther—its habitat was gone almost overnight. The orange groves, cabbage palms, and palmetto scrub, one by one, were succumbing to the big bucks of development.

A prolonged drought coupled with increased water consumption lowered the water table to such levels that salt crept into most home wells, necessitating the use of city water. This water comes from the St. Johns River system, and from deep wells near Bithlo, which is thirty miles inland, aquifers that are also in a precarious state. Commercial clammers come into the area in droves during their off-season up north. These outsiders have no regard for the river and do inestimable damage to the river's grass beds, which are already struggling to overcome the ill-effects of silt from dredging and pollution. These grass beds are inarguably the most vital link in the river ecosystem—they feed all kinds of creatures at the bottom of the food chain and provide shelter for many more. Without them, healthy aquatic life cannot exist in the estuary.

Along with the increased growth came all the headaches of big city living—traffic, crime, pollution. And there was something more insidious—a loss of small town values and the sense of belonging. When Red's mom graduated from high school in the early 1940's, there were twenty-three graduates—from *all* of Cocoa, Rockledge, Merritt Island, and Cocoa Beach! When Red graduated less than thirty years later from the same school, there were seven hundred graduates, just from Cocoa and Rockledge—a thirty-fold increase in as many years.

"Remember when we were children," Red said, "we could safely ride our bikes uptown, leave them (unlocked), go to the movies, and then go to Campbell's drug store for a treat at the soda fountain with the swivel stools. I remember 'Doc' Campbell's had the first automatic door we'd ever seen. We would step on a rubber mat and the door would magically swing open. We kids used to do it over and over again, to the aggravation of the store clerks, I'm sure."

"Anyway, after getting a sweet treat at the counter, which was, incidentally, run by the well-known character and cook Myrtice 'Myrt' Tharpe, we usually went across the street to Mr. Sheehan's bike shop to see what was new, or to buy some bicycle accessory. Like kids everywhere, we used to put playing cards on our bike with a clothes pin so they would flap in the spokes to make it sound like an engine. Aah, simple pleasures for simple minds!"

Red continued, "When we were kids, parents didn't have to worry about their kids getting into trouble or about being harmed: everyone knew whose kid you were, and if you made trouble you can bet your parents would know it before you got home. Now kids go to the mall to 'hang out,' and even in their own neighborhoods, they are anonymous."

Red sighed, "Thomas Wolfe was right, you can never go home."

3 — A Lesson in Proper Architecture

One sultry September day, as we sat on Red's breezy front porch, she discussed the building materials used by our ancestors here in Florida.

"Like pioneers everywhere, early settlers here were good at using whatever local materials they had at hand to build with," Red explained. "For instance, you will find lots of coquina rock in the older houses—they used it for foundations, for outer stone facing, for fireplaces, for sidewalks, steps, and walls around the yards."

"For the main house construction they used lumber that was easy to come by, from local trees they called 'Merritt Island mahogany.' These were actually pine trees, and the wood was called 'fat' pine, something you can't get these days, but which used to be so plentiful it was the building material of choice. Very old, huge pine trees growing locally had large amounts of center heart-wood. This wood was permeated through and through with resin, and the sap-filled lumber was used for everything—beams, floors, doors, and lovely beaded tongue-and-groove paneling. Being resin-filled made it impervious to insects such as termites. It also made it rot-resistant. Years later, when the resin hardens, it becomes impossible to drive a nail into it. All nail holes must first be drilled, and it will dull a very sharp drill in no time."

The resin that made this wood ideal building material for this environment also made it highly combustible—its only drawback. Red frequently recounted how many of these old homes she had seen go up in flames over the years, burning very hot in spectacular conflagrations and being reduced to smoldering rubble in a matter of minutes.

One of the houses she saw burn down was that of "Old Lady Rembert." She was a very peculiar old woman who had a house set back in the over-grown woods and she owned quite a bit of property all around it. Most of it was in citrus trees and there was an old fruit packing house which sat right on the River Road. This became a favorite place for some older kids to paint graffiti—"Hooligans," Red's mother called them. We were all scared to death of old Mrs. Rembert, although she was quite harmless, and we would ride our bikes as fast as we could past her place, for it was a rather long, dark stretch of woods, our over-active imaginations making it much scarier that it actually was. Across her driveway she had a hose like the ones in filling stations, which rang if someone drove over it. This was her alarm system, and when we could get up the courage, we loved to ride our bikes over it, sure that it would be ringing in her house and annoying her.

Her place seemed very spooky to us because it was so overgrown you couldn't see the house from the road, and because she was so seldom seen, Mrs. Rembert seemed a rather spectral figure herself. Short and grey-haired, she wore two braids on top of her head. She was a total recluse, but on rare occasions you could see her out near the road, trying to cut back the underbrush—usually with a pair of scissors. As if those little scissors were going to conquer that jungle! We always dared each other to go up to her house at Halloween, but never got up the courage to do so, partly because of the numerous black cats that freely roamed the property and gave it the aura of a "haunted house." Mrs. Rembert became wheelchair-bound late in life, and one night her house went up in a blaze of fire. She never made it out, being cremated inside her home.

Another local home was built out of a more unusual wood—teak. The Magruders, original Rockledge homesteaders, had a large, fine frame home built of Merritt Island mahogany. Mr. Magruder then built a small house next to it for his daughter. Story has it that there was a ship-wreck washed up on Cocoa Beach. Mr. Magruder took a boat to the West side of Cocoa Beach, then hauled the timber over the dunes and sand to his boat waiting in the Banana River. This fine teak wood was used to build his daughter's little house. Both her house and the original Magruder home are still standing today overlooking the Indian River. Incidentally, this daughter, Sallie, wrote a small book called *Young Pioneers in Florida* about her childhood here. Red's family had a copy of this book in their library.

Whether you are looking at old houses in Savannah, Memphis, or along the Indian River in Florida, from the lowliest "cracker" shack to the stateliest antebellum mansions, you will see common elements in the architecture. Above all other similar characteristics there is the unifying factor that these buildings had to fit in with the environment — our forebears had not yet found ways to conquer their surroundings, so they had to find ways to make the Southern climate bearable. And the single most important consideration was how to deal with the heat. Cracker architecture was without peer in this department, and Red always said current developers would do well to study the old ways, that we could use more "environment friendly" building now.

Red explained how simple it was. "First, trees, nature's air-conditioning, were left in place on a piece of property and then more were planted around the houses. In the South, a yard without trees will bake in the summer, forcing people indoors. Of course, a house with no trees around it will also bake, necessitating that marvel of twentieth century technology, air-conditioning."

One of Red's favorite "theories" was that developers must be in cahoots with the air-conditioning manufacturers. "What other reason could there be to cut down trees in Florida?" she continued. "Unfortunately these days, cutting down trees is something the modern developers with their ubiquitous bulldozers can't wait to do.

"Admittedly, when it's hot as Hades in Florida's mid summer, it is very nice to work in air conditioning, but with common sense, a house can be built to be very comfortable without it. Our ancestors did it all the time."

In fact, Red said that when she was a kid, schools never had air-conditioning — a concept totally unbelievable to Florida kids nowadays.

"Americans are becoming too soft, too affluent, too spoiled," Red said disdainfully.

17

Red didn't have air conditioning in her house. She didn't like it—she said she liked to hear the sounds of nature, and what was going on outside. She especially liked the night noises—the croaking of the frogs, the soft call of the whippoorwills, and the haunting hoots of the owls.

Besides trees, there were several other features of these old homes which made them not only attractive, but naturally cool. On one of those sweltering summer days, as Red and I drove down the river road, she pointed out her favorite houses.

"Look at the graceful wrap-around porches on that old house. That not only provides a great place to sit in your rocking chair, with a good view of the river, but keeps the house cool too. You see, Shrimpette, the porch provides shade and keeps the sun off the side of the house. Another thing, when the afternoon rainstorms blow up in the summer, the windows can be left open because the porch covers them. That allows the suddenly cooler air to circulate through the house, cooling it off. Of course, that means the windows must be made correctly. They must not only be large and plentiful, but placed properly. Old-time builders knew the value of placing windows low and in such a way as to provide cross-ventilation, another cooling feature of these great old houses."

Porches also played an important role in everyday life of Southerners. Not only were they a great place for entertaining, but they were crucial to the flow of information between neighbors. In short, they were the "grapevine" of old timey communications. From your front porch you could see the comings and goings of everyone, and you could pass along whatever was gleaned. Neighbors visited and information (some might call it gossip) was exchanged on a regular basis. It was the very relaxing, personal, and enjoyable forerunner to the telephone and the cold and impersonal E-mail!

As we stopped to visit Red's elderly Aunt Bertie, Red continued her instruction in proper architecture. Even though Red had visited such architectural meccas as the Parthenon, the Blue Mosque, and Char-tres cathedral, I believe she appreciated these old southern houses just as much, if not more.

"Notice the high ceilings. They allow the heat to rise well above head level, thus keeping our area cool. The advent of ceiling fans has helped even more."

"Another feature of these wonderful old places is the ample attic space," said Red, sounding a bit like someone trying to sell a house. "They almost all have stairs to the third floor, which usually was kept as storage space.

Some are actually used as extra rooms, they are so large. Regardless, they make good repositories of hot air. As the house heats up during the day, the hot air naturally rises and ends up in the attic."

Heating the old houses in winter was another proposition. They had no insulation, and the windows were usually very leaky. Most of the original heating systems involved radiators and a water boiler in the basement. Some houses had steam heat radiators, which were quite warm, but in Red's house there were just regular hot water radiators, usually just one in a room. The house never got truly warm. As the water was heated in the furnace boiler, it rose up through the pipes, circulating through the house. When Red's house was "modernized," a central heating system was put in and they removed all the old radiators except one. Red kept one in her living room just to show what they were like.

One winter, after the new system was installed, Red was wishing they had the old radiators back. It was an unusually cold winter, so the heat was on a lot. At night, Red started to wake up, noticing there was a nasty odor in her room. It took her a little while to realize that she only smelled it when the hot air was blowing out of the ceiling vent. Her mother, who did not like heat, kept her air vent shut off, so she couldn't smell it. After two nights of nauseating smells emanating from the vents, Red ventured into the basement, holding her nose tightly shut. Sure enough, there was a dead rat lying on the floor next to the furnace. Red said she'd rather have the old ineffectual radiators again than that smell, to which her mother agreed, because she liked to warm her socks on the old radiators.

As Aunt Bertie went to get us some cool lemonade, we explored the trunks and other treasures in her large attic. In one old steamer trunk we found a long unused ivory and silk fan brought back from Paris by Red's grandmother. Then we found exotic, elegant feather hats, long out of style, which we modeled in front of an old forgotten mirror. We couldn't tarry long in the heat of the attic, though, and we hurried back down to the cool of Aunt Bertie's porch, where the world's best lemonade awaited us. She grew her own lemons and squeezed them herself, adding plenty of sugar for girls with a sweet tooth.

We hated to say goodbye to Aunt Bertie, but a swimming pool was waiting for us in Rockledge. There, on the River Road, Red and I often went to swim in a sulfur water pool with a friend. This girl's grandfather owned a house called "Little Rhody." It was a beautiful little frame house, built in 1921 by Mr. H.L. Myer—of the Myer's Rum business. We often looked in the cellar, as rumor had it that the Myers used it to stash rum they had run from the Bahamas during the Prohibition. We never found anything but some old empty bottles down there.

Red's house, too, had a cellar, a rather rare feature in Florida homes. It was always damp and cool and Red's German grandfather used to make his favorite sauerkraut down there—just like in the old country. He also used to make fine wine down there of an unusual variety. When he went north every summer he would bring back quantities of concord grapes from his brother's vineyards on Long Island. The wine he made from these he combined with grapefruit wine he had made the winter before, which ended up a delicious concoction indeed. Red's mom was always lamenting that he had not left behind that particular recipe.

Continuing her discourse on architecture, Red brought up another important feature of Southern houses, the offset kitchen. Most of the old kitchens now have been incorporated into the main house by modern owners, but Red told me a good example still exists at Marjorie Kinnan Rawlings' home in Cross Creek, Florida. The kitchen sits behind the main house, connected by a covered breezeway. This had two advantages, Red explained.

"First, kitchens furnished with wood stoves used to present a real fire hazard. In the event the kitchen caught fire, (which was not infrequent), it would do minimal damage, usually just burning down the kitchen. That was a whole lot easier to replace than the entire house. Second, as wood stoves put out a lot of heat, the kitchen became a sauna when in use. Separating it kept the rest of the house cooler."

Red continued, "Another practical feature of the old homes was that most of them were built on pillars, raising them off the ground. This helped to keep rodents and termites out, as well as allowing air to circulate under them, having a cooling effect and deterring wood rot. Anyone who has ever lived in a house built like this knows that the canine members of the family love this arrangement: dogs know that under the house is the coolest dirt, and it also offers protection for them from thunderstorms and downpours. In the old days, before the advent of good flea protection, dogs always lived outdoors."

One of Red's favorite rooms in southern homes was one designed to make the night heat bearable. Many old southern houses have sleeping porches—open, airy rooms that are very delightful for resting and reposing. These porches are either screened in or they are all windows, and almost always upstairs. Being up high, these open rooms will catch even the slightest breeze and allow it to blow freely through, using cross ventilation to cool the room for comfortable sleeping on even the hottest nights.

One of Red's favorite River Road homes was that of the Parrishes. This house was built in 1885 for a Mr. Barnes. Some years later, with another owner, it was actually used as a hunting lodge, and called the "Palmetto Lodge." But in our day, the Parrishes owned it. Mr. Henry Uriah Parrish, Sr. was a wealthy grove owner and lived in this grand house close to downtown Cocoa, where his wife, Julia, entertained lavishly, and which is still in his family today. For Red, it was one of the most beautiful examples of Southern architecture in our area. It had a huge front porch, tall ceilings, and numerous stained-glass windows and doors. Inside, it was dark and cool and the woodwork was incomparable—beautifully carved doors, fireplaces, and coffered ceilings.

Red, constantly bemused by the oldtimers' names, joked one day, "you know, Mr. Parrish should have married Julia's sister, Euphemia, then it would have been Uriah and Euphemia Parrish! Wouldn't that have been a pair of names!"

Red's dad told stories about old man Fortenberry's sawmill, which supplied most of the fat pine used for building in our area. The sawmill used to stand on the southeast corner of Courtenay Parkway and State Road 520—which is now the busiest intersection of Merritt Island. After milling the huge pine trees, and cutting lumber from the heart wood, there would be piles of sawdust five stories high to play in. Red's dad said he and his boy chums would get old car fenders or pieces of sheet metal, and using them as toboggans, slide down the enormous sawdust hill. Now there are no pine trees left that big, and Mr. Fortenberry's sawmill has long since been replaced by a bank.

Old man Fortenberry, whose only other name was just "A," owned much of Merritt Island at one time. He was county commissioner during the depression and bought up huge tracts of land for the price of unpaid taxes—often just pennies on the dollar. He bought the land for the timber—the fat pine—on it, although later it became far more valuable to his heirs as land for developing. In spite of his affluence, he lived way up north on the Island on the Banana River in an old shack. Red's dad was pals with one of his sons and would spend the night there, getting up early to cross the street to the river to hunt ducks. There was no wallpaper, insulation, or inside walls at all, and one could see the daylight—and feel the cold winter wind—through the many cracks between the boards. The paved road ran just up to his house on North Banana River Drive and stopped there, continuing as a dirt road. Red said that the original pioneers, people like Old Man A, the Magruders, and the Remberts, were tough, hardy people and used to living like that—they preferred it that way.

"It was people like that all over this country who made it as great as it is—the first explorers and settlers—tough, self-reliant, and hard working people," she said.

Sadly, like Old Man A and his ilk, fat pine is now obsolete. They used it all up, not only here, but in the entire eastern United States. But the beautiful grain of the wood, its strength and durability, combined with the careful craftsmanship of the old builders, made for comfortable, sturdy, and lovely old homes which will outlast us all.

Red always said when a big hurricane came she would ride it out in one of the old houses, because they were built to last, and indeed, hers and others on our River Road had weathered many a hurricane.

4—"He's No One-Stone"

One of Red's family's favorite and most used rooms in their old house was the library. It was lovely, dark and cool, and ceiling-to-floor bookshelves covered the walls. What an unusual and eclectic collection of books it contained! It was the collection of four generations—herself, her father, grandfather, and great grandfather—of book readers and accumulators. Not only were they a family of superior intellect, they were also very well-educated, and their book collections mirrored their varied interests. These were not people who just bought books for collecting, or to impress people; they bought books, read them, and kept them in their library.

They were so well known as readers that people would give them their book collections, before or after they died. Among others, Mrs. Minnie May Myers, Red's dad's English teacher gave him her collection just before she died. The estate of Dr. Walter Page also gave her dad many of the doctor's books, and the widow of another doctor in town gave Red her husband's medical books after he died.

Sometimes I would house-sit for Red when she was away on one of her many trips, and I would use the time to sit alone, unbothered, in her library, pulling books from the shelves one at a time. I would leaf through them and try to absorb some of their contents. And I realized, as Red used to tell me, quoting from Shakespeare, "There are more things in heaven and earth, Horatio, than are dreamt of in your philosophy."

Red and her library changed my life forever.

Often, on our bike rides to downtown Cocoa, Red would take me into Mr. Ellinor's bookstore. She would save her pennies and buy books for her dad for Christmas. Mr. Ellinor was also the projectionist at the State Theater across the street from his book store.

One thing that helped make Red an avid reader was the fact that her father would not allow a television in the house until she and her brother were off to college. TV was new back then, and of course, all the kids agitated for one, especially Duncan. But her father was adamant, and he knew what he was doing. She was only allowed to go to the neighbors' house on Sunday nights for the Disney show, "The Wonderful World of Color." Duncan, on the other hand, would sneak over to the neighbors every chance he could to watch the boob tube. He did not become a big reader until later in life.

Later, Red would say how grateful she was that there was no TV in her house to stifle her imagination or to replace her precious books. In fact, she thought TV one of the most pernicious influences in our culture. Not only were a whole generation of ignorant children being robbed of their own imaginations, of outdoor activity, and all the concomitant pleasures associated with open air, but a whole generation of lazy parents were using the boob tube as a baby sitter, robbing their children of the pleasure of reading books.

There were also other ills associated with the TV. Red complained bitterly that TV was selling "the American Dream" of over-consumption and living beyond one's means with their clever and subtly influential advertising. A whole generation of kids glued to the boob tube saw endless commercials of "beautiful people" living a dream life—of endless spending to have more "stuff" and of conspicuous consumption—an unreal world that supposedly anyone *could* have and that everyone *ought* to have.

Red thought if you see something often enough, you begin to believe it. That also applied to the violence on TV that was to come later. There was no doubt that these TV-addicted kids would become inured to and would emulate the blatant profanity, the open sex, and the continuous violence paraded across their TV screens. Sadly, this has come to pass, and parents don't seem to have the power or the inclination to get rid of the televisions, and now, the computers filled with internet pornography.

Why should they? Not only are the TV and computer their most useful baby-sitters, but the parents are addicted to it also. As Red predicted, we have become a nation of boob tube ignoramuses. When Red encountered one of these uneducated idiots who thought he was so smart, she would wink her eye at me and say, "He's no one-stone, that's for sure," which was her secret way of saying, "He's a dolt," for "one stone" translated into German is *"ein stein. "*

Red's father was a true "renaissance man," for, in addition to his great love of learning, he was also a sportsman, an athlete, and a builder. There was practically no book he would not read and absorb. He was a true wealth of knowledge and information, and there seemed to be no subject that he didn't know something about, and most subjects he knew a whole lot about. Erudition could have been his middle name. Red used to say, "My dad has forgotten more than most people ever know."

Red and her father had not only lots of native intelligence, but were highly educated as well, her dad insisting on a broad, well-rounded, liberal arts education for his children. Red thought it was a disgrace for good minds not to be well educated. She had numerous college degrees—her father called her "the perpetual student." In spite of all her book learning, she thought the primary aim of higher education was to teach people *to think for themselves in the light of reason,* critical analysis, and logic, and without emotion. As she explained, "would you rather someone, say a doctor or a politician, make an important decision based on logic, facts, and objective reasoning, or on subjective, emotional feelings?"

One could always look up facts and figures in books, she said, but to be able to analyze problems and facts and draw conclusions based on rational thought was what you should learn to do first. After you learn to do that, learning the facts comes easily. Of course, she said that this idea was not original with her, this had been the purpose of Plato's academy in ancient Greece.

Red said, "That's one problem with so many people today—they don't know how to think for themselves, so they fall for any slick sales pitch, any smooth talking politician, any glib con artist. Instead of questioning these people, they just eat up whatever they are fed. You know, Socrates said that the unexamined life is not worth living, that we need to be critical and self-critical. Shrimpette," she admonished me, "be a One-Stone, and question everything, including yourself."

Besides being well-read, Red's dad could fix almost anything, and he could build anything. This suited her mom because she didn't like to throw anything away. If it could be fixed, it would be. That family was the definition of frugal. They deplored waste, "planned obsolescence," and the "throw away society" we were becoming.

My favorite memory of their creative recycling was a fly swatter "invented" by Red's German grandfather. It was a ruler-sized stick with a well-worn shoe sole nailed to it. It was certainly effective against the ever-present roaches and flies. Decades after the old man's death, it was still hanging on its special nail in the kitchen.

Like Red's grandfather, she and her dad were always working on "projects." Red was full of ideas, mainly for the yard, and her dad was a willing, though sometimes a dubious, helper in her many and varied projects. After all, her projects always seemed to turn out pretty well and were an asset to the property. You never knew what they would be building next: bat houses, topiary yard art, fountains, bird houses, elaborate vine-yards, or beautiful ponds. Her dad would run electricity for her and taught her how to lay pipe. She knew her way around the wood shop too, using the table saw, drills, and other tools when she needed to. Like her father, she became a jack-of-all-trades, something that perhaps rather intimidated her boyfriends.

Inside the old house Red and her dad also had endless projects. At one time or another Red refinished most of the antique furniture therein.

"Look at this, Shrimpette," she exclaimed, "a beautiful mahogany *armoire*, underneath four or five layers of old lead paint! My grandfather painted every stick of furniture in this house. If only he knew how much work it is for me to uncover it all—stripping, scraping, peeling, and sanding—it takes lots of elbow grease."

And it *was* beyond belief that someone could paint over all that beautiful wood: bird's eye maple dressers, oak tables, walnut tables and sideboards, oak cabinets and desks. Red enjoyed laboriously removing the many coats of decades-old paint and bringing these beautiful old pieces back to life. Red said it was fun to discover what kind of wood was underneath.

So Red and her dad were partners in the fixing up of the old house, for there was always something that needed fixing or installing. I think part of what drove them to be fixer-uppers was an intellectual curiosity—in order to fix something, one had to understand how it worked. So they would take it apart, figure out how it worked, then fix it if possible.

Red's brother also had an inquisitive mind and was a "project person." Even as a small boy, he was always building elaborate tree houses, go-carts, river rafts, and forts. His ability to acquire junked wood and other free building materials greatly expedited his building endeavors.

Red guessed they came by their project and fixer-upper mentality genetically, as not only their dad was an able fixer and builder, but her German grandfather had been also. Not only did he make the famous family fly-swatter, he fixed everything that needed it around the house, and he did some beautiful woodworking as well. If you lived in an old house, it was definitely a valuable asset to be able to fix and build things yourself, for, as Red would say, "The only thing that works in an old house is the owner."

5—Fish Tails

Red came from a long line of anglers. One of the earliest photos I remember seeing of Red is of her Mom and her on the end of their old cement dock, fishing. Red was holding a cane pole three times longer than herself, patiently waiting for the next fish to come along. I learned from them that fishing, like many other things in life, is a very diverting and relaxing hobby; and besides that, you get to eat the fish. I was always thrilled whenever they invited me to go fishing with them.

Red's mom told me about the time when Red was very small and while fishing off the dock hooked a very large black drum fish.

"She began to yell, while bravely trying to hang on," her mom related. "That huge fish was heading north and the line was buzzing. If her dad had not come to the rescue, that big fish would have pulled her right in— as little as she was, she still wasn't about to let go of that fishing rod."

This was in the pre-monofilament days, the fishing lines being made of thin string, and the open-faced, level-wind reels were very primitive by today's standards and rather difficult to cast.

Now, non-fishermen don't realize how fishing becomes a true rite of passage for a kid. When you are little, they give you a cane pole to use: it is simple, safe, and relatively difficult to mess up. At a certain point you begin to badger the powers-that-be to use a "real" rod and reel. But first, you must master the art of casting, not an easy thing for a little kid, and much more difficult in the old days. The old, conventional reels required a great deal of touch and finesse: not enough pressure of your thumb, and you would get a backlash—a big snarl of fishing line. Too much pressure with your thumb, and your cast didn't go very far. When Red was learning, she practiced for days casting a hookless, weighted line in her driveway. Many years later, she helped me do the same.

When casting was mastered, and you had graduated to the rod and reel, you had arrived, you were somebody, you magically grew two feet overnight! You were not a little kid anymore, you could now fish with the big guys.

Red's mom loved to fish off their dock, hoping to catch a speckled trout for her dinner. In the early days, that was no problem; later, it became difficult to catch "keepers"—fish big enough to meet the legal size limit. Then she mostly caught little trout, too small to keep, or catfish. She told us how the trout fed close to the surface, and how you can tell if one had bitten because they always went for the head of the shrimp, and that part would be quite mangled.

Catfish, on the other hand, are bottom feeders, and if you let your bait get too deep, that's what you would catch. They are difficult to de-hook, as they have sharp, poisonous spines on their dorsal and lateral fins. Most fishermen leave them out of the water to die instead of throwing them back, regarding them as "trash fish." However, their relative, the "sail cat," which gets quite large and is fun to catch, is tasty to eat.

Red's dad was a good storyteller, and Red, especially, liked to listen to his stories. Even at a young age, she seemed to sense that, as wonderful as it was for all of us living when we did, it had been even better when her parents were growing up on the river. That was when things were wilder and people were freer and there was room to move.

One day Red's dad told us a story about when he was a teenager. The old causeway across the Indian River was built on wood pilings with crossbraces. He climbed out and sat on the braces, bare feet dangling in the water. Holding a hand line near the pilings, he was angling for sheepshead. This particular day had been a good one, and he had a pretty good stringer full of the pretty black and white striped fish. Seeing a commotion in the water below, he looked down to see, with fear and amazement, a huge shark grabbing all his fish. The beast was a good eight feet long, with a head almost two feet across. With his heart pounding nearly out of his chest, not only did he pull his feet out of the water right quick, but he nearly fell off the cross-brace, trying to maneuver to a higher position. Some years after that, a tiger shark was caught in front of the old Indian River Hotel, making headlines in the local paper.

When we were kids, there were still many small sharks in the river, which locals called "sand" sharks. Everyone who fished would catch them from time to time. They traveled in schools and never seemed to get large or cause anyone harm.

Red and I used to turn over rocks at the water's edge to find fiddler crabs. Menacingly, they would wave their little claws at us, and Red explained this is how they got their name—they looked like they were playing the fiddle. Fiddler crabs just happen to be one of the sheepshead's favorite snacks, so we would bait up our cane poles and start fishing. If we were having no luck, we would scrape some barnacles off the dock pilings, "chumming" the sheepshead, as this was another of their favorite foods. When we caught them on our cane poles it was a lot of fun, as they put up a good fight and were very pretty with their black and white stripes.

Redfish, or red drum, locally called "spot" fish, also were around the rocks in abundance. They were fun to catch and good eating too. Now there are strict size and number limits on redfish and there are not as many to be found.

One of the strangest creatures we used to catch was the eel. Sometimes they would bite a hook, and that was one strange looking fish to pull in! Black, slimy, and snake-like, they looked far more vicious than they were. In Europe and other places people eat eels, but we always threw them back. I don't know if there are any eels left in the river any more.

I also wonder about the curious, elegant little sea horse. They were so fragile and dainty, we would catch them in little minnow nets, keeping them in tanks overnight to observe them, then putting them back in the river the next day.

Whether or not the fish were biting, Red and her Mom just liked being down at the river, always with the dogs, taking in another beautiful sunset, or watching the dolphins, (called porpoises by locals), play. Of course, when the dolphins showed up, the fishing was over for the day, as they scared all the fish away, hunting for their own supper.

"The porpoises have to eat too," Red would say.

One quiet evening we were down on Red's dock and a pelican came gliding by—right "on the deck," as pilots would say. Pelicans fly like this all the time, and it always mystified me how they could so effortlessly glide just inches over the water without beating their wings or falling into the water.

"Pelicans use very effectively what aviators call 'ground effect,'" Red explained—she always seemed to have an answer to my questions. "It all began with a Swiss physicist named Bernouli. He discovered that as fluids move around an object, the fluid—in this case, air—on the top of the object—in this case pelican wings— is at a lower pressure than that on the bottom. The pressure differential, and the higher pressure on the bottom gives the object 'lift.' This is how airplanes take off, and also how sails pro-pel sail boats. Not only are pelicans using lift, but by flying very low to the water, their bodies and wings are compressing air between themselves and the water, making the pressure even greater than usual underneath them, keeping them aloft. This is called *ground effect* and airplane pilots, just like pelicans, make use of it when flying very low to the ground."

Red really liked pelicans. Coming back in from fishing in the ocean with her dad she always fed the pelicans their leftover bait. Used to receiving handouts, they became pretty tame out at Port Canaveral.

"Most of the 'beggars' are juveniles—all brown, with no white or yellow on their heads," Red noted. "Many of them never learn to hunt and dive for their food, the way brown pelicans are supposed to. This is because so many people feed them."

She wondered what would happen to them when people quit feeding them. She likened them to people on welfare—as long as they were on the dole, there was no incentive to work for their food.

She then reminded me of the old maxim, which she stated in a more pertinent way, "Give a pelican a fish, and you feed it for a day. Teach it to fish and you feed it for a lifetime."

Red's dad also was a great fisherman. He liked to fish in the ocean, and was one of the most knowledgeable anglers I've ever known. Honed by years of practice and keen observation, his ability to locate and land sportfish of all kinds was wonderful. Red loved to go out with him, rising before dawn and hitting the ocean by daybreak. Sometimes they would take me or her brother along too. However, her brother didn't really have the patience for it and preferred hunting. Red, on the other hand, was an avid fisherman and would sit patiently waiting for a bite. Her face would beam when she reeled one in and her dad would say, "Why, Red, you're a regular Izaak Walton."

When I asked her who Izaak Walton was, she explained that Walton, born in 1593, in England, was famous for his book about fishing, *The Compleat Angler.*

Mostly Red's family went out fishing in their boat from Port Canaveral, just south of the "Cape" where the rockets are launched. But they also took fishing trips to the Florida keys, to the Gulf at the Suwanee and Crystal Rivers, and to other points on the East coast.

In the winter, bluefish run in the surfline off Cape Canaveral and they used to come home with large coolers brimming over with "blues." To catch them, they trolled back and forth, within sight of the missile gantries and the historic lighthouse, painted with black and white horizontal stripes, which was on the point of the Cape.

Red used to play a trick on their out-of-town visitors that the family took fishing with them, telling the visitors that the lighthouse was a missile sitting on the pad waiting to go. Most of them believed her too: as she often laughed, "Yankees don't know any better."

Florida doesn't get the huge bluefish that are caught up north, but when they are plentiful and feeding, they will strike almost anything you throw in the water, and every line will have one on it. Catching them with little outfits (light tackle) is the most fun, and when you're catching hundreds, it's quite hectic and exciting.

Red's family never kept more than were wanted, and Red went door-to-door in the neighborhood giving them away. Blues are rather strong tasting fish, but if you bleed them out as they are caught, they are quite edible.

Often we saw birds circling overhead, indicating fish, and that's where we hoped to find the lovely, orange-spotted Spanish Mackerel. They also were fun to catch on the little outfits and very delicious to eat.

Back in the fifties, in the early days of the space program, there was a missile called the Snark. They had so many duds that ended up in the ocean that it was a common joke to refer to the ocean off the Cape as the "Snark-infested waters of Cape Canaveral."

Actually, they *are* shark-infested, the waters of Cocoa Beach and vicinity being second only to Australia in numbers of sharks. Not uncommonly, swimmers and surfers got nabbed by sharks in the surf, and they still do.

Red's dad told us about when he was a boy of seven living in Melbourne Beach, around 1930. He had a friend from the mainland, Richard Best, who used to come over almost daily. The boy's mother, who had polio, would go swimming in the pool at the "Casino" for therapy, while her husband and son, Richard, would go to the beach. Red's dad, who lived at the beach, would usually join the father and son, who was about twelve or so. Melbourne Beach at that time was undeveloped and beautiful in its wild isolation, with just the "Casino" where people would change clothes, then go to the beach or enjoy the two sulfur water pools.

One particular day, Red's dad had been naughty and was not allowed to join his friend to play at the beach. The day was calm and sunny, the ocean like a millpond. Richard and his father were in chest-deep water when Richard exclaimed, "I've been stung."

His father, thinking it was a jellyfish, told him to go rub some sand on it, until he noticed blood welling up in the water. He pulled his son out of the water, loaded him into his big Packard car, and drove him to the hospital in Melbourne, at least a half hour away. No one ever knew what the predator was for sure, but it was presumed to be a large, hungry shark. The boy had a huge chunk taken out of his abdomen and pelvis and died quickly. When Red heard the story, she said, "I guess sometimes it pays to be bad," referring to the fact that her dad was not there because he had been naughty that day.

Years later when Red and her dad went fishing in the ocean, he said he still didn't like sharks. So, if the fishing was lousy, he and Red would troll around and catch sharks just for the fun of it. Catching the powerful sharks provided an unbeatable workout, and even though she was in good shape, Red would complain she was sore for days afterward, as even a small, two foot shark would take her a half-hour to land.

When the ocean was very calm, they would go offshore to the reef, about twenty-five miles out, where the depth was ninety feet or so. Here they caught king mackerel, also called kingfish, and in years past, they used to catch a lot. Now, like everything else, there is such a small limit on the kingfish that it is hardly worth going that far. But they are a wonderful sport fish to catch: stream-lined and muscular, they are good fighters and have flaky, white meat, which is tasty to eat.

In the summer there is usually little wind and Red and her dad would go offshore looking for dolphin. If out-of-town company were going along, they would be aghast at the thought of catching "Flipper," until Red explained that the dolphin fish was quite different from the mammalian porpoise. If you can find a weed line or any large floating object, you can usually find dolphin underneath. Gorgeous blue-green fish, the smaller ones, called "schoolies," all stick together, a definite advantage for the fisherman. Red used to feel sorry for them, because when you caught one and left it on the line, its friends hovered around it and you could catch many more at once.

The larger "bull" and "cow" dolphin travel alone and will be picked up at random while trolling. Typically weighing forty or so pounds, they are beautiful to watch, as they are magnificent jumpers. When you finally land one, their lovely blue-green color fades to yellow, and it makes you kind of sad. Also called Dorado and Mahi-Mahi, fresh dolphin fillets are some kind of good eating.

Red loved those fishing trips, even if they got "skunked," for there was always something interesting to see: sea turtles, giant manta rays, flying fish, porpoise, or sharks. If nothing was biting, she would scoop up sargassum in the landing net and investigate it for sea life. The seaweed was a microcosm of the whole ocean: in it, you would always find baby shrimp, small crabs, tiny file fish, or box fish.

Red learned all kinds of good fishing lore from her dad — how to look for birds feeding, usually meaning fish feeding too; how to put out chum and teaser lines; how to spot the magnificent frigate bird, a sure sign that fish were near; and last but not least, when the fish weren't biting, how to spit on your bait to bring the fish. Any good fisherman knows that.

6—Siestas

One of the joys, determined by necessity, of living in the tropics, is that of the afternoon siesta. Now, most people, when they encounter this particular facet of a peoples' lifestyle, jump to the erroneous conclusion that it is born out of laziness. This is not usually the case.

Taking an afternoon siesta is a worldwide phenomenon found among those peoples who are lucky enough to live in the sub-tropical and equatorial zones, and also in many Mediterranean countries. It is not necessarily a symptom of idleness, but rather a very practical and time-honored way of dealing with the climate. Except for Florida, no hot climate in the world has the luxury of ubiquitous air-conditioning. Most Mediterranean countries only have air conditioning in office buildings and hotels. True tropical countries, mostly considered "Third World" have very little air conditioning at all to speak of.

In the heat of the day in the tropics, unless you are fortunate enough to work in air conditioning, you are forced to rest in whatever shade you can find. The unrelenting heat and sultry humidity of the tropics are so overwhelming you have no choice. As Noel Coward once remarked, (only) "Mad dogs and Englishmen go out in the midday sun."

So, typically, people in these climates eat a big noon meal, have a siesta, and begin to stir only as the afternoon cools off. Then they return to their work and stay at it until late evening.

"It just makes sense when nature dictates your behavior not to fight it," Red commented. "In this country, we have overcome the elements to a degree with the widespread use of air conditioning."

But not Red. She lived in one of the old houses which to this day does not have central air conditioning. She would wake early and had her chores finished by mid-morning when it really began to heat up. You could usually find her mid-day on her front porch, reclining on her antique wicker swing or in one of her numerous hammocks, waiting for the sea-breeze to come up. She would be stretched out languidly with an eye mask over her eyes, snoozing away. She believed that when your eyes are closed, your other senses become more acute, and this was one reason she disliked air-conditioning. With windows closed and the noise of the air conditioning, one cannot hear the wind in the trees, the peaceful lapping of the river' waves, or the expert imitations of the mocking bird.

"Air conditioning is just one more way modern 'conveniences' have divided us from nature and made us less in tune with our surroundings," Red declared.

Even when she was older, she was an ardent advocate of open windows and the "siesta system," a gentle and pleasant way of life all but extinct in this country. Indeed, I believe she made it into an art form. It also served as a method of meditation for her, and you never knew, under her eyemask, if she was asleep or simply cogitating on her day's activities or life's subtler points. However, she always awoke revitalized, her brain and body recharged, and she usually went out to her yard to do some pruning, weeding, or perhaps fishing off her dock. And so her life flowed, one day into the next, her dogs at her side, awaiting the next adventure.

Finding her on her glider always brought to mind Wordsworth's poem about daffodils that she used to recite:

> ...For oft when on my couch I lie
> In vacant or in pensive mood
> They flash upon that inward eye,
> Which is the bliss of solitude.
> And then my heart with pleasure fills
> And dances with the daffodils.

That was Red at her finest, lollygagging on the front porch and spouting poetry.

7—Battling the Bugs

Fighting the elements in Florida was never easy, especially in the summer. The sultry summer afternoons with their sopping humidity and enervating west wind cause a palpable ennui with life so intense as to be inescapable. One usually becomes acclimated, in time, to the heat, the occasional hurricane, and the violent thunderstorms, but the insects are a different story.

"Between the mosquitoes and the roaches, it's enough to drive a saint to sin," Red used to say.

Red's mom used to tell stories about the 'skeeters in her day. They were the same blood-sucking, voracious pests we know now, there were just a whole lot more of them.

"Our screen doors would literally be black, covered with a live, buzzing blanket of bloodthirsty insects. A person entered and exited the house very quickly, so as not to let them in. We kids would run as fast as we possibly could down to the Whaley's pool and jump in before we were devoured by the hungry bugs. Then we'd keep our heads under water as long as we could hold our breath," Red's mom said.

Very few of these old-timey pools still exist. They were built of concrete above ground (there was too much coquina rock underneath to be hacked away by hand for an in-ground pool), and filled with sulfur water. Sulfur water comes from artesian wells deep in the ground, four hundred feet or so, and doesn't need to be pumped out of the ground: the water is under sufficient head to rise above the containing aquifer and so it simply flows to the surface under its own pressure—hence the name "flow wells."

Red had a sulfur water well on her property, as did all the grove owners. The water was used to irrigate the citrus trees and to fill the spray rigs. She and her brother loved to drink it, and she claimed it was healthier than regular water, being full of all kinds of minerals. Most people today are sickened by the stuff, proclaiming that it smells like rotten eggs, but old-timers grew up on it and most still prefer it if they can get it. Red also believed that it helped repel fleas on her dogs when they drank it, and they seemed to prove it so, for they had very few.

"I drink sulfur water, and I don't have any fleas either," Red's dad would joke.

Red's property also had two of the old water towers that everyone had on their property. These were water cisterns to hold rain or well water, then used in the house and yard, using gravity for pressure. The problem was, if you had a two-story house, there wasn't much gravity available to get the water to the second floor. Water trickled out of the upstairs showers. There is only one water tower left on our river road now, one last curious vestige of a different era.

Red's German grandfather was an avid card player. One night he and some of his cronies were playing a nice game of bridge when Red's mom, then a girl, decided to play a joke on him. She and a friend ran down the road knocking coconuts together, in a cadence similar to a horse's trot. Her father, thinking the old grove mule, John, had escaped, ran outside. The front door was left temporarily ajar, and the house filled with hungry mosquitoes. It was the only time she could remember her father losing his temper, he being a man of great patience and a sweet disposition. Why, he didn't even get that mad the time Red's mom snuck into the cellar and shook up the beer bottles. When he served it to his guests, his foamy, home-made beer spouted out and hit the ceiling. Anyway, after the mule prank, no one slept much that night, Red's mom said, except the satiated blood-sucking mosquitoes.

'"Skeeters were a fact of life then, and pretty much all year 'round too. Of course they were much worse in the summer," Red's mom told us.

One August was particularly memorable. It was, as Red bemoaned, "as dry as a catfish that's been caught and left in the sun to die."

In what was supposed to be a very rainy month, day after cloudless day passed by without rain. Then September rolled around and with it, heavy clouds full of moisture. Portentously, Red said, "we were better off without the rain, because now the mosquitoes will come."

And come they did. All the eggs laid during the drought on the edges of ponds, mudpuddles, and streams hatched, and surely the mosquitoes were as thick as they had ever been in the history of Florida. When walking on the grass, great puffs of them would rise up, covering your legs. Even at midday you would be swarmed, which was unusual for the daytime. Our screen doors were covered with them, and Red reminded me this was what it was like every day in our grandparents' time. In the days before window screens people slept under mosquito netting at night and slapped and swatted them all day.

Although the mosquitoes are pretty much under control now, it's unlikely the roaches in Florida ever will be gone.

Like most people, Red had a real aversion to roaches, but it was more than that, she was downright terrified of them. Spiders, snakes, and other vermin didn't bother her, but roaches gave her nightmares. She wasn't alone, as we had some pretty huge specimens of roaches in these parts. The old frame houses stayed fairly infested, especially in wet weather.

One day a violent storm blew over a cabbage palm in Red's yard. Since it was on the ground, Red's mom had the heart cut out and dined that night on heart of palm (called "swamp cabbage" by locals).

Her mom always maintained she could very easily live off the land, and she did so most of the time. Together with a ripe avocado off her tree and fresh stone crab claws she trapped in the water off the dock, with key-lime juice squeezed on them, she made her lunch. Red's dad said the Queen of England didn't eat that well, and I believed him.

Anyway, when that palm tree hit the ground, hundreds of huge, fat, ugly, glistening brown palmetto bugs scurried around, like rats abandoning a sinking ship. And palmetto bugs have the extra unpleasant feature of a nasty odor they emit when bothered. Luckily, they can't fly like the cockroaches.

No one who has lived in these old Florida houses has escaped the nocturnal terror of being awakened from a sound sleep by a roach crawling over arm or face. They are thoroughly disgusting creatures, and it doesn't make it any better knowing they will be here long after the human race has done itself in.

When Red would get particularly disgusted with the way things were going in Florida, with the "northern immigrants" and the developers, she would say, "Florida will only be fit for the cockroaches soon. Let the Yankees have it."

8—A Trip to Bonnet Pond

Red took me one time to her family's lake cottage in the center of the state. It was a small frame house dwarfed by huge live oaks and hickory trees of obviously venerable age. Ferns grew on the upper side of the huge branches, and Spanish moss hung from the bottom. They provided deep shade, and the graceful moss blowing in the breeze made them positively enchanting and endearing — gentle giants with long grey beards. In the twilight, great horned owls and barred owls would glide noiselessly and land on their great limbs. The lake was clear water, albeit brown colored. Great, old, vase-shaped cypress trees grew out into the water. The lake bottom was sandy, perfect for swimming.

In late summer, huge schools of large, black pollywogs would swim near shore, delighting kids and dogs alike. Wading through them felt like walking though cooked macaroni. They were about five inches long and very soft and squishy. These were the tadpoles of the river frog, common in north Florida lakes and rivers. As they matured, legs would appear at the base of their tail, then would continue to get longer and bigger. Eventually the tail would drop off, and they would miraculously change into frogs.

It was here that I learned to "grunt" for earthworms, which were used to catch fish — shellcracker, bream, and shiners, which the next-door neighbor paid us to catch for him to use for bass bait. Red's dad showed us how to grunt for worms. In a damp, shady corner of the yard, he hammered into the ground a two-by-four board, putting it down about two feet or so. Then he took a piece of two inch pipe and rubbed across the board, much like rubbing a bow on a fiddle. The results were astonishing — trying to get away from the vibrations, big, red earthworms came to the surface and crawled on the ground, where we commenced picking them up. The nice fat wrigglers would make good bait for us later that evening, when we hoped the fish would be biting.

One day we took the canoe on what Red said would be an "adventure." Paddling down the lake we saw huge birds' nests high up in the stately

cypress tree tops. Presently, a beautiful osprey flew over, fish in its talons, and only then did her babies' heads appear at nest edge. Ripping up the fish, she fed them and flew off again, crying her shrill call. She circled back behind the tree line over what I supposed to be land, and we could hear her calling from further away. Then Red said, "It's just here that we turn in."

I could see nothing but a dense wall of water weeds, trees and brushy growth, but as we drew closer, I saw a small cut through the solid line of bushes. It looked like a tunnel, with light at the other end, and appeared to be fifty feet or so in length. Luckily, the water level in the lake was quite high, or we couldn't have made it through. In the small canal the water was almost too shallow to be passable, and we grunted and sweated while poling our canoe through. Grabbing onto the underbrush, we pulled and heaved ourselves along, not wanting to get out and portage, as the bottom was mucky here. If one were claustrophobic, this would not be the place to be. Mosquitoes kept reminding us that we could not tarry, but had to get on with the job.

At last we came fully out into the bright, steamy daylight of the peatbog that Red called Bonnet Swamp. The water here was clear and the color of a brownish port wine. The solid peat bottom was only six inches or so below the water, but who knows how deep it went; Red explained that the tannic acid given off by the peat gave the water its distinctive color. Voicing my trepidation about swimming in acid-water, she calmed me by saying, "Every time you drink tea, you are drinking tannic acid. It is the same that imparts its color to this water. It is a very weak acid, and old-timers say it will toughen the pads of their dogs' feet. Hence hunters often soak their dogs' feet in tea to toughen them up before going into the woods."

We poled easily with our paddles across the broad expanse of reeds and lily pads. It occurred to me that I had never been in a swamp before, and it truly was a magical place. Far off to our right we could see a great blue heron, standing as if frozen in a Chinese painting, stalking its lunch. On a raised cypress root, a snapping turtle sunned itself, slipping off noiselessly into the water as we drew near. Overhead the ospreys circled, shrieking and looking for baby food. The water lilies were in bloom and I could see why Red considered them her favorite of all flowers. Their beauty was breathtaking, and we were surrounded by them, by reeds, water, and nature. Red could identify the animal life and all the swamp plants, the pickerel weed, *saggitaria,* yellow-eyed grass, and cattails.

She then pointed out the plants with the globular yellow flowers. "Those are called 'bonnets' by the locals, and that's how this swamp got its name, but their real name is spatterdock. This particular type of biome, or habitat, is the most productive of any biome on earth— swamps produce tons of plant and animal life, constantly."

I had never before been totally surrounded by the wild, and it was almost overwhelming. In the eerie silence it seemed sacrilegious to speak. We sat very still for a while in our small canoe, just taking in the stunning beauty of it all, talking in whispers. Although I did not realize it at the time, some-thing about that place would stay with me all my life: the smell of a fresh water swamp. It was such an earthy, clean, pungent yet subtle smell, so different from our salt water river smell. To this day when I am near the lakes and rivers of Florida the similar scent evokes memories of that day long ago in Bonnet Swamp.

We took out a cold drink, as we had worked up quite a thirst getting from the lake into the peat bog swamp. Red laid back in the bottom of the canoe and rested her drink on top of a lily pad. "Organic table tops," she said, bemused. Soon the sultry heat forced us to take up our paddles again, pol-ing our way to I knew not where. But I was sure that Red did. We crossed the bog to another line of trees on the other side. If the first trip through the small cut from the lake was difficult, this was ten times so. At one point,

Red had to get out in the muck and pull the canoe along. Right about then, I thought Red was the bravest person I ever met.

Red said this was our labor pains and I didn't understand. After pushing, sweating, and grunting for fifteen minutes through this small, root-filled, mucky passageway, I finally understood, as we were "born" into a deep, cool, inviting lake. The labor pains had been worth it. This was Bonnet Pond, an almost perfectly circular, clear reddish-water lake.

When you dived into it your skin looked like an Indian's, so red was the water. It was completely ringed by cypress trees, and, as the pond was surrounded by the swamp, there was no land suitable for landing.

So we slipped over the side of the canoe, ever watchful for alligators and water moccasins. Our sweaty bodies relished the refreshing, clean water. It was just us in our own personal, private lake, with maybe a snapping turtle or two for company. We swam and lazed there for quite a while, then reluctantly made our way home the same way we had come. Upon arriving back at the big lake, we again cooled ourselves with a dip. It had been an unforgettable day on Bonnet Pond.

9—The Secret Life of Chickens

Although Red's grandfather originally had a flock of Rhode Island Red laying hens, they were long gone, and Red's family had a "hobby flock" of bantam chickens, actually inherited from a neighbor. This neighbor was a doctor, and it so happened that one of his patients could not afford his services. The patient paid his bill with a pair of bantam chickens, prompting Red's dad to quip, "I wonder if the good doctor declared them as income to the IRS?"

Over the years those chickens had migrated to Red's yard because her family liked them and fed them. They were pets, but they were really wild animals, hiding their nests all over the place and roosting in various trees at night. Red's mom in particular enjoyed messing with them, and they jokingly called her the "Chicken Lady of River Road."

They *were* beautiful chickens, small and feisty, but not vicious. The roosters were usually bright orange, with iridescent blackish-green tail feathers, although some roosters were silver and gold color instead of orange; they all looked like game cocks. But not one was ever known to attack anyone with their spurs like many roosters will do. The hens were a plainer blonde or black; occasionally a white one was hatched and they were highly prized by the family because of their rarity.

Believe it or not, those were some pretty smart chickens, if there is such a thing. We used to watch the rooster helping to choose a nesting site for the hen. After a suitable place was found, he would stand guard nearby while she laid her egg—usually one every other day or so. And how those banty hens loved to have babies! Red explained that the broodiness was never bred out of them, like the commercial laying hens. Their one great desire in life was to be a mama. Every day was like Easter over there, as Red's mom would offer a dime to anyone who found a hidden nest. Even when she took all their eggs away, those hens would keep on sitting, sometimes for weeks on end with no eggs in the nest, so badly did they want babies.

When Red's mom did let them hatch out, how proud they were of their new broods, strutting around, showing them off, and getting all huffed up if anyone or any animal came too close. The tiny biddies looked like little bugs running around and climbing on their mother's back. They learned very quickly how to scratch for food, take dust baths, and eventually, fly up into the trees to roost at night. As a kid, Red would be fascinated watching the chicks hatch—first "pipping" a small hole in the hard shell, then using what must have been for the tiny chick a Herculean effort to enlarge the hole, sometimes taking all day. Then the chick would emerge all wet and wobbly, glad to be out of its very cramped quarters.

Often Red would help them along, delicately peeling off some of the shell to make it easier for them. Her mother told me that when Red was a small girl, late one afternoon she came into the house after playing with the just-hatched chicks, where her mom was preparing for a dinner party. Red was covered from head to toe with chicken lice and began itching all over. Luckily the doctor next door came to the rescue, and Red was scrubbed down with lice soap, just before the guests arrived.

"I hate to be nit-picking, Red," her dad said, "but you are one louse-y child!"

And if baby chicks are cute, baby ducks are even more adorable. Sometimes Red's mom would get some duck eggs and put them under a hen. After sitting on them for four weeks, instead of the three weeks it takes for chicken eggs, the hen would have her reward: some very large and funny

looking chicks! When Red was a little girl, her mom would catch the ducklings and put them in the bathtub with Red, where they looked like peeping wind-up toys.

The mama hen would just about lose her mind when those baby ducks headed for the river, for as all ducks do, they wanted to be in the water. One time, the hen flew in after them and Red had to fish her out with a net. She was sopping wet and just about to drown—what a mother bantam won't do for her biddies! And it always confounded the hen why, at three weeks of age, those ducklings couldn't fly up into the tree to roost. They had tiny, undeveloped wings compared with chicks the same age, and had much larger, heavier bodies. There was no way they could get up into the trees. Raising baby ducks was a real trial for those little bantam hens.

For a while, Red's family had chickens, ducks, and a beautiful peacock. We used to love to watch him strut around, displaying his gorgeous tail feathers. Red called him Rex, for his bearing was so regal. Poor guy, he was always strutting for the chickens, and I don't think they were ever impressed, but we were. It was always a special occasion to find one of the "eye" feathers that he had shed around the grove somewhere. We would save them as a special treasure, delicate and beautiful as they were.

Many years later, after Rex was gone, someone gave Red a female pea-fowl, or peahen. She had a gimpy leg from a youthful injury and limped around the yard, trying to keep up with the chickens. Red's mom wanted to call her Stumpy, but Red disagreed, tongue-in-cheek, "You know, the latest vogue is 'self-esteem,' and we wouldn't want her to feel bad about herself. 'Stumpy' might give her a complex and she could become psychotic—her name will be 'Queenie.'"

She was beautiful, too, and the little upright feathers on top of her head prompted one of their typical, off-beat family debates: were they tiny jeweled rays of a beautiful tiara, or an avian version of a Las Vegas show-girl's hat?

That Queenie, however, was a real pain when any hens hatched out a brood of biddies. She was fascinated with the little chicks, and would follow them around, and, cornering them, would just stand and stare at them, driving the mother quite mad. Red theorized that she wanted some of her own, but they weren't about to get her a mate to find out.

One day, I heard a big ruckus over in their yard and saw their white Peking male duck chasing a hen. Chasing the duck was the peacock, and chasing them all was their dog, Shadow. I think he had finally gotten fed up with all the fowl in his territory.

Sometimes the chickens got bold and pecked some dog food out of his dish, while he was lying there seemingly asleep. He would let them get really close and then simultaneously growl and lunge at them, precipitating what sounded like the third world war. You never heard so much cackling and carrying on—it was bad enough for a Labrador retriever to tolerate birds in his yard, but eating out of his food dish was more than he could bear.

Around that same time, Red was raising an orphan chick. Its mother and brood-mates had all been killed by some kind of varmint. One biddy was left, and Red called the baby "Yahooty." She would carry that biddy around, kissing it and talking to it and it would follow her around like a dog.

Well, Shadow didn't cotton much to the whole situation—Red was *his* buddy, and he didn't want any stupid chicken interfering. He knew better than to kill that baby, but he would look on with scorn and disgust as Red played with Yahooty. One evening the family went out to dinner and poor Yahooty was never seen again. Not one feather was ever found as evidence, but Red's mom always suspected Shadow. He did have a certain smug look about him, and he sure was a lot happier having Red all to himself.

The roosters thought themselves very handsome, which they were, and would routinely fly up on the fence to crow, first facing one way, then turning and crowing the other way. Red said they were like all males—vain and show-offs. After all, she said, "where do you think the word 'cocky' comes from?"

After the hens laid eggs, they would start cackling (Red said actually they do that to call the roosters over to mate with them, thus fertilizing future eggs), and the roosters would join in the cacophony. They would cackle loudest of all, as if they had anything to do with the laying of that egg! But they sure acted as if they did, and they always strutted around putting on an air of bravery. Yet they were always the first to run for cover if a predator showed up. So much for the brave roosters protecting their flock.

Kipling said, "The female of the species is more deadly than the male," and it was certainly true in the chicken yard. Unlike the craven roosters, the hens would show no mercy if something attacked their biddies. Some would actually land on a dog's head, pecking furiously, the dog high-tailing it for safety! They scared away many a cat and dog, just running at them, attacking, all ruffled up to twice their size, proving once more, as Red quoted, "the best defense is a good offense."

Those tiny banty hens were very brave and very intimidating when their babies were threatened, and many of them gave up their lives protecting their young.

"It just goes to show," Red averred, "there's nothing stronger than mother-love."

Later in the 1970's when feminism came into vogue, Red expressed concern about the effect this would have on the American family. One day while in the garden, we stopped to observe a mocking bird attacking her black lab, Polly. Poor Polly, she could not escape the wrath of this little bird, as the mocking bird kept swooping down on her, chasing her away from the bird's territory. She had a nest in an orange tree nearby and didn't like Polly anywhere near her babies.

"You know," she said, "we could learn a lot from the birds and other animals. As a biologist I can say that probably ninety-five percent of the males in the world have but one role to play: to contribute their genes to the next generation. That is why the strongest males are the ones who get to breed — to ensure that their offspring will be as strong as possible, thus helping their survival rate and thus the survival of the species. There are a few exceptions, notably some birds and seahorses, but most males in the animal kingdom have no connection with their offspring after breeding."

"Therefore, it falls to the mothers to rear the young. It is clearly obvious to any scientist that the role females play in ensuring the continuation of the species is to raise the young safely and successfully to adulthood.

"It's really quite basic: the male contributes strong, healthy genes, the female protects and nurtures the young till they are grown. This is nature as it has been for eons, this is what is dictated by the way animals are made, and these roles are largely dictated by chemicals called hormones. Males have testosterone that makes them physically stronger and aggressive, thus being able to fight for the right to breed. Females are guided by estrogen, which makes them caring, nurturing, and protective of their young."

"What we as humans need to glean from studying the 'lower' animals is that females are natural caretakers. This is why I believe that children need their mothers more than anything, to keep them safe and secure until adulthood. As Fred Mertz said one time in I Love Lucy, 'Why, Ricky, men just aren't cut out to be mothers.'"

"Why can't the feminists see that — that the woman's place is truly in the home. I believe that their movement is detrimental and really devastating to the American family. They tell the American woman that she *can* have it all—but that is simply not true. I have no problem with a woman being educated and having a career, but if she chooses this path, she should not have children. If she does, the children should be the top priority. The bottom line is that we *cannot* have it all. The children are the ones who suffer from the neglect and the worn out mother who has bought into this fallacious dream. And I am tired of those who say that the mother has to work nowadays to help support the family. Sometimes it may be true, but I see how most of these people live—they buy every imaginable material possession for themselves and their children, to make up for the time not spent with them. The children would be better served with less stuff, and more parental attention. I am so thankful that my mother stayed home to raise us. She was always there for us, and was never too tired to help us with homework or to sit up with us if were sick in the night." Red sighed, "If we would just understand, accept, and follow our biological nature, the human race would be a lot better off. Like the baby chicks and mocking birds, children need their mothers, *all the time,* until they are grown."

Red thought it ought to be that way for humans because that's the way it was in the wild and in the barnyard.

In her "barnyard," when the baby chicks became young adults, the pullets, or young hens, would start laying. More often than not, the first eggs they laid were very tiny, the size of song-bird eggs, and sometimes they would have no outer, hard shell on them, just a tough membrane keeping them from breaking. They had been formed incompletely due to the young age of the hen.

Those banty hens were pretty good layers too. The eggs were small, and the yolks were an unusually dark orange color. Red explained that was because they were free-range chickens and ate lots of different things— weeds, seeds, and bugs. They also loved tomatoes, cooked eggs, and any kind of organic kitchen garbage. Between their dogs and the chickens, no food ever went to waste at Red's house.

As "teenagers," the young roosters, or cockerels, would begin to crow. When you first heard them, they sounded like some kind of sick or choking animal, then they would graduate to sort of half crows. Eventually, they would develop a full-blown rooster crow, although some were always superior crowers to others.

When Red's dad was a boy, growing up on Merritt Island during the depression, a neighbor of his raised chickens. Red's dad struck a deal with him: he would supply him with catfish to feed the chickens in exchange for eggs. He duly went about his job of catching catfish, delivering them daily to the egg man. But the first time they had some catfish-fed chicken eggs everyone gagged and turned green—the eggs tasted like fish! Needless to say, that bartering deal didn't last too long.

Red's dad's family also had a deal with some other neighbors once—they purchased a milk cow together and the neighbor boy would milk it in the morning, and Red's dad would milk it at night. He told us, "One time I was milking that cow and a fly started buzzing around her head. Then, all of a sudden, it flew into her ear. Presently, as I was pulling on the udder, along with milk, out came that fly! It was a real case of 'in one ear and out the udder!'"

One September day Red called me over, all excited about something; I had to come right then or I would miss it. I ran over and their family was in the kitchen hovering over the table, on which sat a single egg. I was thinking, "all this excitement over an egg?" when I noticed it wasn't behaving like a normal egg—It was standing on end. I thought it must be some kind of trick, that it was glued there. It wasn't, and her mom explained that that day was the fall equinox, and that at a certain moment, and for a very brief window of time—about five minutes—eggs would stand on end. It was true, and I was duly impressed, as were we all.

Red's Mom was the uncontested chicken lady; it was true that from years of observation, she seemed to know everything about the habits of chickens. Sick chickens, however, always posed a challenge. Whenever one was acting puny, Red's dad generally proclaimed, "That chicken's got the pip," his diagnosis for just about everything to do with sick chickens and kids.

Red and her mom, however, tried to doctor them as best they could, putting antibiotics in the water or catching a chicken if it needed more serious treatment. One time an old rooster got really listless and quit eating. He got so weak he couldn't grip the branches at night when he went to roost. Red caught him, put him in a box, and gave him water and liquid food with a medicine dropper. She also, as many farmers still do, gave him an injection of several things mixed together. The next day he was strutting around as if nothing had happened. An older neighbor down the street was very impressed and said, "Do you think she could give me a shot of that stuff?"

As new people moved into the neighborhood, and it started to be less "in the boonies," sometimes these "city folk" would complain about the noisy chickens. For they did as all chickens do—they crowed loudly and long in the early morning, and sometimes new folk didn't appreciate that kind of alarm clock. Then the animal control guys would come around and knock on Red's door. After stating that the chickens would have to go, Red's mom would tell them that the chickens were wild, and if they could catch them, they were welcome to them. They always left scratching their heads, and they never did catch the first one, or even attempt it.

When there got to be too many roosters in the flock, it became a real problem. The ideal ratio was about one rooster to six hens; if there were too many roosters, they would harm the hens with their aggressive breeding. One time an ad was run in our club's newspaper: "Free Roosters—Beautiful. All you have to do is catch them. Good for alarm clocks."

The guest room in Red's house was in the back, right next to the trees where the chickens usually slept. Guests were awakened at the crack of dawn. Red's family slept through the racket, as they were accustomed to it. Red's dad said there was a reason the guest room was there—after a few early mornings, people were usually ready to leave. The chickens made sure guests never overstayed their welcome!

Red, of course, loved the chickens, but being an avid gardener, many times cursed her "foul" fowl. As anyone who has free-range chickens knows, it is very difficult to have a nice yard and gardens with chickens around. Those wild chickens of theirs must've had the toughest drumsticks in all poultrydom, as they spent all day scratching for food. Too many times they scratched for seeds in Red's flower and vegetable beds, prompting her to threaten to wring their scrawny necks. She claimed they never ate enough bugs to offset the damage they did otherwise.

When they weren't digging up her plants, they were lazing around taking dustbaths. Now, there is hardly anything more satisfying than watching a bunch of chickens relaxing at a nice warm dustbath. They had their favorite spots—always exposed sand in the sun. They would lie down and roll around in that warm sand, using their wings to fluff the sand through their feathers. Then they would lie there for a while longer in the shallow, bowl-shaped holes they had made in the dirt, soaking up the sun and warmth from the ground, eyes closed, napping. Supposedly, archaeologists have found those little pits made by chickens in their dust baths in very ancient digs around the world.

"That goes to prove," Red said, "that chicken behavior hasn't changed a bit through the millenia."

Those chickens at her house had the good life, for sure, and probably would've overrun the whole neighborhood, had they not had lots of predators.

Red's most unusual Christmas gift had to do with—what else?—a chicken. One summer the great horned owls had been particularly bad, killing many of the chickens in her flock. One evening, hearing a ruckus outside, Red ran out to the orange tree where the chickens were roosting. Her beautiful, young, gold rooster fell out of the tree, into her arms—dead as a stone, without a mark on him. The owl had attacked him and, as birds will, the rooster had died of fright. It so happened that Red's young nephew was learning the art of taxidermy, so she put the hapless rooster into her freezer to give to him. When she next saw him, she told him, "Now practice on some other birds, then if you do a good job on this poor guy, I'll pay you for your work."

Red forgot about it and did not see the bird again.

That Christmas, out trooped her nephew, proudly, with the stuffed rooster! However, he had not studied chicken stature and had mounted it in a flying position—it looked like a pheasant with a big red comb. His once beautiful, shiny, black tail which he held up so proudly in life was droopy and straight! Not only that, but obviously her nephew had not quite mastered the technique of removing all the flesh and tissue, so the lovely rooster was extremely malodorous. To neutralize the odor, the boy had poured a bottle of cheap after-shave on him—the combined effect of the necrotic flesh and cheap perfume being very noxious. With stuffed specimen in her car, Red and Polly both rode home with their heads hanging out the window.

"That was the sweetest gift I ever got," she told me that evening, "but not the sweetest smelling!"

One time the flock got down to just a couple of roosters and hens. For the first time we'd ever seen, the hens weren't really interested in the old red rooster, even though he was the top in the pecking order. Red thought it was because the gene pool had gotten so small, that he was inbred and very stupid, and the hens were smarter than he was.

Red's mom swore that if he hadn't already fathered some biddies that she would have thought he was "gay." We all laughed at the thought of a gay rooster. It was a fact, though, with his droopy tail, floppy comb, and scrawny physique, he wasn't much of a *macho* rooster. The hens would not even follow him up in the tree at night, preferring to choose their own roosting spots—highly unusual behavior for chickens. However, that scrawny old red rooster was definitely top dog, somehow intimidating the other younger, larger rooster into being afraid of him.

Unfortunately, despite his pluck and moxie, he was a dud in the fertilization department. Eggs fertilized by him were only about 30 percent likely to hatch, where the other roosters typically had 80-100 percent fertility rates.

Believe it or not, at the same time, one of the hens started crowing. No one would believe it, until several people heard her, trying to crow, sounding like a young rooster just learning. Red's mom said she remembered one other time that a hen crowed. Red surmised that perhaps the hens were feminists and were becoming liberated. Now we'd heard everything—gay roosters and feminist hens. What next?

10—Varmints

It so happens that EVERYTHING likes to eat chickens and their eggs. Red said her chickens had so many predators that Chaucer must've been thinking of them when he wrote of his "Small fowl...that sleep all the night with open eye." For if they didn't sleep with their eyes open, they would surely be eaten.

Red's dogs were pretty good at keeping other dogs and any number of varmints out of the yard, but all too often something would get a chicken. Red said her dogs were the self-appointed chicken protectors because they loved to eat the eggs—they had a vested interest in those chickens. If they could locate a hidden nest, they would eat every egg in it, prompting her mom to call them "suck-egg" dogs. She said that's why they had such shiny coats.

One particular dog of hers would very daintily take the egg and carry it around—you couldn't even see it in her mouth! Then she would drop it on the ground, and bite a tiny hole in it, enlarging it until she could slurp out the gooey contents; that dog ate eggs so fastidiously that she never spilled a drop!

Red's family didn't mind the dogs eating the eggs, but took a dim view of any dog chasing and eating the chickens. Only one of her many dogs she could not train to leave the chickens alone. She tried everything to break that yellow Lab of eating the chickens. She even tried the old "chicken around the neck" trick—a chicken the dog had just killed was tied around her neck and left there. Wouldn't you know, that dog let that chicken hang there until it got good and ripe—then she ate it! That dog also loved avocadoes, and we would find her dog house full of avocado pits, where she had brought the succulent fruit to eat it. She and the other dogs that would eat avocadoes always had nice shiny coats during avocado season—Red said they were very good for their skin and coat.

Neighborhood cats would also attack the baby chicks when they could, but left the big chickens alone. Red's dogs did a good job of keeping the feline predators away, always enjoying a good cat chase. Her dogs were also pretty good at keeping the 'possums and 'coons from getting the chickens at night when they were roosting in the trees.

One night a raccoon got in the nesting area after a setting hen. From the tiny building (actually Red's old playhouse) came horrendous sounds, as her Lab had found the varmint and was going to it with that 'coon. I'd never heard such snarling, barking and carrying on. I'm not sure who won, but the 'coon did leave, and the dog finally backed off to nurse his wounds. Many's the night when her dogs' barking would wake me up and Red would tell me the next day the dog treed or killed a 'possum after the chickens. You never knew with 'possums — at night when her dogs attacked them, you would swear they were dead, to find them gone in the morning. Their "playing 'possum" was a very effective defense strategy, even fooling the dogs, for once they appeared to be dead, the dogs lost interest.

Very late one full moon night I awoke to the sound of Red's dog, Polly, barking. As I lay and listened to it I heard Red calling the dog softly, so as not to wake the neighbors. The dog wouldn't stop barking, instead escalating her ferocious woofs to a feverish pitch. Wondering what it was this time, I arose to investigate and found Red in her nightgown down on her dock. The moon was so bright that it almost seemed daylight. As I approached, I could clearly see what the commotion was all about: Polly was swimming in the river, barking, at times inhaling water, then sputtering and coughing. The object of her wrath was a huge raccoon, also swimming around in circles.

Polly had chased it into the river and was swimming between the 'coon and the rocks so it couldn't get back to shore. Round and round they went, coon hissing, dog snarling. Polly didn't care if she drowned, that raccoon was not going to get by her and back to shore. Meanwhile, Red was calling Polly, to no avail, and throwing pebbles at both of them. I laughed so hard that I couldn't believe the whole neighborhood wasn't awake. Red finally threw her hands up in desperation and went back to bed, leaving the dog and the 'coon to work it out themselves. The next morning when I awoke, I wondered if it had all been just a dream, but Red verified that it had indeed happened.

Once Red's mom went into the playhouse to gather the eggs and a large "chicken" snake greeted her, lying in the nest with the tell-tale lumps of eggs in its belly. Actually, that happened fairly often and at night they would crawl under a hen with biddies and eat them one by one, the hen usually oblivious to any genocidal doings underneath her. Of course, these "chicken snakes" were really yellow rat snakes.

"In these parts, anything that eats chickens is automatically given the scientific name of 'chicken'" Red explained. "It doesn't matter if it's a red-tailed hawk or a yellow rat snake, it will become a chicken hawk and a chicken snake!"

One day I wandered over to Red's yard to find her in the little chicken house. She was standing, arms akimbo, looking intently into an empty chicken nest. "Hmmm, this is so very odd," she muttered, "I keep putting fake eggs in these nests, and something keeps taking them out. Not only that, but I keep finding them all over the yard. Very strange."

Red would put egg-like objects in the nests when she took out the real eggs. This kept the hens laying. She explained that if you removed all the eggs from a hen's nest, she would abandon it and go elsewhere. So she used a lot of golf balls, some marble eggs, ping-pong balls, anything to fool the hens. Now they were disappearing from the nests and as she gardened in wild parts of her yard, she was finding these ersatz eggs in the weeds. Could it be the crows, famous for thievery of man-made objects, or maybe playful raccoons?

Some time later, she finally got a "big break" in the case and she was able to solve the mystery. One morning Red found a hen stone dead on the floor of the chicken house, with not a mark on her. The eggs that had been under her were gone. Red knew what sneaky predator this had to be, so she laid in wait. She knew, by the nature of the beast, that it would not return the next night, or maybe not the next. But she checked the nest every night just the same. She had put a fake egg and a real egg in the nest to be sure it would come back. Just as she thought, the wily critter returned on the third night. When Red checked the nest, there he was, and he had already ingested the golf ball.

"Well," Red thought, "I'll put you in a box and release you far away from here tomorrow."

The next day, Red opened the box to show me the thief-in-the-night, and low and behold, that rat snake had eaten the egg and thrown up the golf ball. It still had some semi-digested food on it. Not only did Red catch her hen killer, but, by accident, her mystery fake-egg thief had been revealed. It turns out those snakes could and did eat all kinds of weird stuff, and when their gullet told them it was non-digestible, they would just throw it back up.

One rare and beautiful snake that we saw occasionally was not a chicken eater, though it could have swallowed an adult chicken whole—the huge indigo snake. It was so black it looked blue, and was very long, and very thick—as big around as a man's arm. It certainly looked like something from another place. Its size cannot be over-emphasized, as it was so much larger than any other snake in these parts. When you first saw one, you had to gasp in disbelief that a snake of such size actually lived near you. They are now protected as they are very rare, and it is always a special treat to see one. Not only are they very beautiful, but they are very easily tamed and non-aggressive, making them a favorite of snake collectors.

Red said she never saw an indigo snake eat chickens, but everything else sure seemed to. The one predator that her dogs couldn't ward off started visiting one hot summer night. We were in the kitchen and heard the hair-raising squawk of a chicken in the death throes. We rushed out to see a huge owl flying off with a chicken in its talons. The silent predator was never heard by the unwary hen, as it noiselessly swooped down and plucked her out of the top of the grapefruit tree where the chickens roosted at night.

Another night, under the same tree, Red's dog took off after some kind of shadowy critter sitting on the ground. It turned out to be another great horned owl, and as it took off, it let go of a wounded and frightened chicken it had been sitting on. It had to jettison its heavy quarry to become airborne quickly, as the dog by then had a mouthful of its tail feathers. Red took the poor hen in and nursed it back to health. Its entire back was de-feathered and macerated from the talons of the great bird.

One afternoon, Red's mom saw a beautiful hawk sitting on the ground under the avocado tree. Thinking it was injured or ill, she approached. As she did so, the hawk took off, and a trembling hen which had been totally covered by the bird, ran for the safety of the bushes. This "chicken hawk" was a red-tailed hawk, a beautiful raptor, an efficient and deadly hunter. Such was life and death in Red's back yard.

I went to see Red one day and found her utterly despondent. Her little flock of chickens had dwindled down to a dangerously low number, and the night before something had killed her only surviving rooster.

"Every night lately the chickens have been attacked—by all sorts of the usual varmints," she announced. "One by one, my latest batch of biddies has been decimated."

The final blow came when her red rooster was killed.

Red didn't blame the wild predators; there was a more insidious reason her chickens were becoming extinct, and it wasn't the four-legged varmints responsible for it this time, it was the two-legged type. Because of local development all around her property, Red had a little five acre oasis of citrus grove and wild land, the only undeveloped property for miles around.

All the wild animals were being crammed onto her property, and she unwittingly was providing them with live chickens and fresh eggs to eat. It wasn't their fault: they were just trying to survive with very little habitat to support them. Red said it was that way all over Florida for the wild animals.

Dejectedly she said that she would probably leave Florida when the chickens were all gone—if it was too crowded for chickens, it was for her too. We all knew we would miss those chickens, but it was becoming impossible to save them.

11—Mr Tan

Before Red's Mom assumed the title of "Chicken Lady of River Road," there was an odd old geezer who held the position of "Chicken Man" in our neighborhood. No one seemed to know much about him, except that he had some family "up north." He was a stooped, wizened, little Chinese man, with a shock of grey hair falling on his forehead, with wire rimmed glasses below, usually sliding down his short nose. Somehow he ended up on the doorstep of our neighbors, and they kindly took him in. He stayed in an old shack on their property, actually an old fruit-packing house, which sat in a bamboo grove overlooking the river.

Red remembered going inside his simple home.

"There was a single, bare, old dust-covered light bulb, of no more than forty watts, hanging from the ceiling. It was a good thing the light was so dim, because the place was dilapidated and full of junk! His bed was covered with old newspapers, and he had a small refrigerator, usually with not much in it but little bantam chicken eggs, all of them with dates carefully written in pencil. This is how he knew how old they were.

"There was no indoor plumbing; he had an outhouse out back. Nowadays, the 'code enforcement' people would certainly evict him, but he seemed happy enough—after all, his life was very uncomplicated, and he was living on some choice water-front real estate with a million-dollar view!"

He did some grove work for his landlords, and messed with the chickens—who were his friends, roommates, and often his dinner companions—when they ended up on his plate.

At that time, many of the chickens lived in his yard, and some actually lived in his house with him. One never knew on walking in how many chickens would fly out. He collected the eggs when he could find them, and every so often, he would butcher and pluck a chicken to eat. "How, exactly, he ate them, I don't know, as he had no teeth, and those chickens were so tough you could stew them for a week and it'd still be like gnawing leather," Red said, laughing.

I didn't believe Red that a decapitated chicken would actually take off running till I saw it with my own eyes one day when Mr. Tan butchered one.

"Which proves," as Red said, "that a lot of those old adages, like 'running around like a chicken with its head cut off,' have their basis in fact."

After beheading it, he would dip the unlucky fowl in a pot of boiling water, to facilitate removal of the feathers. After plucking it, he would eviscerate the bird, ending up with one very tough, and very scrawny carcass. It seemed to me like an awful lot of work for very little reward.

Now, this little Chinaman's name was Mr. Tan-Saipan, but we just called him Mr. Tan. Sometimes, while jumping rope, we would sing-song, "Mr. Tan, chicken man, likes his chickens in the pan. Mr. Tan, China man, sleeps with the chickens when he can."

Late one night, as often happened, the chickens were raising a ruckus out in his back yard where they roosted. Mr. Tan got up to investigate what was after his beloved birds. In the darkness, he caught sight of a shadowy varmint and gave chase to the critter—in his birthday suit, I might add—and got a very rude awakening. It was a skunk, and it let go and sprayed him from head to toe. The usual remedies were brought around by all the neighbors—tomato juice and all kinds of soaps and shampoos. I don't think he'd had that many baths in the last five years. Red's Mom contributed some Octagon soap, but all efforts were to no avail. How he stunk for weeks after that—your nose could always tell where in the neighborhood he was!

One day he told us he heard a chicken squawking in his back room the night before. That was where they nested to hatch babies. The culprit happened to be a yellow rat snake, called a "chicken snake" by the locals. Usually these hungry reptiles would just swallow the eggs, or the very young babies, but on this occasion, he had found one wrapped around the poor mother hen's neck, and had to laboriously and gently unwrap it from around her, all the while trying to avoid being bitten himself.

Red explained, "Most people don't realize this type of snake is a type of constrictor, and can kill its prey just like a boa."

Eventually Mr. Tan passed away and we went to his funeral. Out of respect we wore our Sunday best—frilly cotton dresses and patent leather shoes.

He looked even smaller than in life lying there in that big casket. The next day he was shipped up north to be interred with his kinfolk, whom we had never met.

"I'll bet he misses the warm Florida sand buried up there in that cold northern earth," Red said wistfully.

We always liked Mr. Tan and we missed him. We missed him even more when the bamboo grove was cut down and a new, modern-looking house was built where he had lived—another little piece of our childhood had been chipped away.

12—The Cyanotic Scion—a True (Blue) Lady

I don't know if it was because of her family's European heritage or not, but Red's whole clan was into cards. They played all kinds of card games: primarily poker, pinochle, cribbage, and bridge, but occasionally rummy, casino, and canasta as well.

Her great-grandparents used to come down from New York in the winter and were avid poker players. In fact, the old man, her great grandfather, was such an aficionado that he had three identical poker tables made: one for his New York City residence, one for his summer mansion in Trenton, and one for his daughter's (Red's grandmother's) house in Florida. These were massive, and very beautiful oak tables, with tops that came off to reveal the smooth green felt and the wells for chips underneath. Many enjoyable nights several generations of Red's family spent at that table, ceiling fan whirring overhead, chips clicking, and cards shuffling on the table below. One night in the winter of 1926, after a game of poker, Red's great grandmother went upstairs to lie down with what she called "dyspepsia." She never woke up.

"She probably lost a bundle of money, and it gave her a heart attack," Red mused.

Red's German grandfather was a widower and had a great many "lady friends," as they politely called them in those days. Mostly they were a group of sweet little old biddies, including my grandmother, who played cards with him on a regular basis.

So vivid is my memory of one of them that I shall never forget her. She had the quaint moniker of Miss May C. Quinby, and everyone called her "the blue lady."

As most old people do, she had very thin skin, and one could see her veins quite easily. This gave her slender, white hands a blue tinge which always intrigued us. Coupled with her aristocratic mien, her blue-toned skin led us kids to believe she was "blue-blooded," hence we thought she must be royalty.

"She had a congenital heart defect, which led to poorly oxygenated blood, thus giving her skin a blue, or cyanotic hue," Red explained to me. "They used to call people like her 'blue babies' at birth. Nowadays those heart defects are surgically corrected right away, but hers never was."

Perhaps this was the reason she seemed perpetually cold, and always wore a cashmere coat with a fur collar, even in warm weather.

Weighing less than a hundred pounds, fur coat and all, this diminutive lady was always immaculately dressed in a beautiful hat, white gloves and a full-length dress—this as late as the 1960's! She was a true gentlewoman, the kind of elegant lady one reads about in Victorian novels, an honest-to-goodness living anachronism, driving her antique car into the dawn of the space age.

Miss Quinby had a little curio shop called "The Women's Exchange" on Barton Avenue in Rockledge, around the corner from her house. There she sold knick-knacks, sundries, and antiques. Her home was a huge Tudor-style house on the river that her father had built. He was a wealthy businessman from Cleveland and the family spent the winters on the Indian River. But as curious and wonderful as she was, what really intrigued us kids was her car—every bit as much out of a time warp as she was.

Parked under her carport, in mint condition, there was an ancient electric car! It was a beautiful, shiny, dark green 1903 Baker, manufactured in Cleveland, Ohio. It ran on a dozen or so batteries made by Thomas Edison. In fact, Edison was the first person to purchase a Baker automobile, and it was the first car he owned. These cars were popular for their elegance and their quiet, smooth ride.

They were especially popular with women, as they had no difficult crank to start them, they were very clean, and they were virtually noiseless. They had a driving range of about fifty or sixty miles before the batteries needed recharging, which was plenty for most women driving around town, certainly enough for Miss Quinby. Her car was a tiny, one-seater, and seemed to be built just for the tiny lady who drove it. It really did look like a carriage without horses.

It was always a special event to see Miss Quinby driving in her little car. The little lady and her unique automobile were sure-fire traffic-stoppers and head-turners. People would do double-takes in disbelief when they saw that shiny green car and the blue lady inside.

Miss Quinby often played cards or visited with Red's and my grandparents, parking the car on the road in front of our house. Then Red and I would check out her most wonderful auto carriage. It had real head lamps—beautiful, brass and glass lanterns with small bulbs in them. The light produced from them was so faint Red's dad used to say, "You'd have to strike a match to see them."

The car was operated with a hand stick, or tiller, and it had little window shades that one could pull down—which we did—and they would spring back up. One time we pulled one down, and could not get it to go back up. We were so worried that she would scold us, but she never said a word. She was used to kids playing with her little car. On Sundays while she was at the Presbyterian church, she would pay a couple of local boys to wash it. Knowing that she was occupied in church for a while, they usually took the liberty of taking it for a spin around town. She surely knew about these escapades, but never got after them.

One day Red and I were coming across the causeway into downtown Cocoa, when, to our dismay, here came Miss Quinby—on the busiest one-way road in the county—going the wrong way against traffic!! We watched with bated breath until we saw her pull off onto a side street. She was pretty old and dotty then, and shouldn't have been driving, I suppose, but as long as she stayed on the River Road, we knew she was safe enough.

It wasn't too many years after that that she quit coming down in the winter, and we heard that she had passed away. Miss Quinby, an only child, never had married and so was the last of her line. We felt sad—with her demise, the end of an era had come to pass. I often wonder how dear little Miss Quinby would survive today. Her electric cars, for she had a second one up in Cleveland, though coveted by many, ended up in a museum there.

Many years later, electric cars were recognized for their environment-friendly qualities and were experimented with once again.

"Perhaps Miss Quinby wasn't backward at all, but really on the cutting edge of technology," Red mused. "After all, she was 'environmentally correct' before it was fashionable to be so!"

13—Merritt Island Mullet Chokers and Other River Rats

As in most small towns, we had our share of characters, town drunks, and nutty dowagers, and it seems quite a few with unusual names, which Red always got a kick out of. And Red's family contributed their share of crazy kinfolk to the town's eccentrics too. Besides Mr. Tan, Mrs. Rembert, and Miss Quinby, there were many other unusual people in our area, who were all part of the colorful mosaic of our young lives.

One such character was Alvah. He was from a family that had a dairy farm and grove on Merritt Island. Alvah's father was Swedish and worked his boys very hard from a young age. The father himself also worked very hard, clearing the land by hand and planting groves and gardens. They also raised chickens and milked cows, and thus were largely self-reliant.

It was Alvah's job to milk the cows and deliver the milk, even as a small schoolboy. Now, Alvah was always rather goofy and silly as a kid, and stayed that way all his life. Presumably he was named for his mother, whose name was Alvaretta. Alvaretta was herself a character. As many women of that time, she hand-made all her clothes, from hats to underwear. She could and did make everything except her shoes. Her hats, which she was never seen without, were well known, being large and well adorned. As a side business, she sold commercially made corsets, and she always wore one, even on the hottest days.

Red's mom went to school with Alvah, and during World War II he was a very popular boy. This was because everyone lived on food rationing coupons, but if you were friends with Alvah, you could buy extra butter and milk from his family.

Later in the 1960's, Alvah and his brother, now both adults, and their mother, moved from the farm to the other side of the river. They still had the groves, but now lived together in a large frame house on the river, where his mother rented rooms. This house had a feature that all the kids thought was "neat."

It was an elevator chair attached to the stair railing. Alvah used it daily to go up and down the stairs.

Living here on our River Road, Alvah became known for his really eccentric behavior. He was yet another "chicken man of River Road," for he had a pet rooster that would perch on his shoulder. Alvah and his mother both had antique Packard cars, and Alvah with that rooster on his shoulder would drive around town, attending town council meetings and other events. One time, he hand-painted a sign nailed to a palm tree in front of his house that read, "Deer Crossing." The fact that there were no deer for miles around didn't seem to matter.

As kids, we delighted in Alvah's antics, but we never knew that they usually were fueled by drink. Poor Alvah and his brother, too, were diligent drinkers. Besides alcohol and the rooster, Alvah had two other passions in his life: radio talk shows and beauty pageants. He would sit in his room for hours, listening to radio talk shows. When he was gassed enough, he would call into the talk show, where the host knew him very well as a regular caller.

Now it so happened that one night his next-door neighbor, a high-school girl, was having a slumber party. Late that night, she and her girl friends went for a dip in her pool—*sans* clothing. As luck would have it, the pool was almost right under Alvah's window. He had been tippling rather heavily that night and he just had to call into the radio to apprise them of the situation. The girls' skinny-dipping episode got very good airplay, and one can imagine what their mothers thought—if indeed they ever knew.

As for his other passion in life, whenever he could, Alvah would go alone or with a friend to beauty pageants. The highlight of his trip would be a picture of himself with a beauty queen. He loved being photographed with the beauties, and had some of these pictures displayed on his wall. He also carried pictures of these girls in his wallet, which he would show off to his male acquaintances. Alvah also attended the nearby Presbyterian church regularly, sitting in the back pew telling ribald jokes to his old codger friends. Alvah, his brother, and their mother all died within a year of each other and the old house was sold.

One of Alvah's close neighbors on our River Road was an elderly matron with the euphonious name of Euphemia. She was the sister of Julia Parrish (married to Uriah). In the typical southern way, everyone called her "Aunt" Feemie. She was famous—or rather, infamous—for making orange wine. Unfortunately, it was so awful—more like vinegar—that it was undrinkable. You knew it was going to be a long and trying afternoon when she invited you in for a "glass of wine." Red's mom got stuck many times at Aunt Feemie's with a glass of the terrible stuff. Poor old Aunt Feemie must've thought her guests had the weakest bladders in town, as they were always making excuses to go to the bathroom, where they could surreptitiously pour her wine down the sink.

One day Red and I were at the swimming pool of her friend Buzzy, who lived next door to Aunt Feemie. He swore Aunt Feemie showed him once a trap door in her closet. When he lifted the trap door, he could see in the darkness a cover, made of metal or wood, like a manhole cover. Aunt Feemie told him that was the cover to a tunnel that led out of the house to the river. Hers being one of the oldest houses around, the tunnel was put there so they could escape if Indians attacked. Our eyes grew wide and we wondered if Buzzy was pulling our leg. He swore it was true but Red got to wondering. Most likely Indi-

ans would come in canoes from the river, so the escape tunnel would lead right to them! We never investigated Feemie's closet or looked for an outlet at the river, so it remained a titillating mystery.

Another River Road neighbor was Uncle Joe. Uncle Joe was a short, little, wiry, old German who had been in the Alaska Gold Rush. He lived in a trailer in the back yard of his nephew's home. Uncle Joe was an extreme recluse and a very talented artist. Red's family had some of his paintings and loved them. He was not at all partial to kids, and if they were making too much noise in the grove behind his house, he would get out his shotgun and threaten them. He always had his shotgun out on Halloween night, thwarting any trick-or-treating at his house.

There was a billy goat that lived in the grove behind Red's mom's. Like Uncle Joe, he didn't much cotton to kids either. Of course, Red's mom and her friends used to tease him until he would chase them around the grove, horns lowered, eventually making them seek refuge in a tree. There he would stay, keeping his young tormenters treed, sometimes for hours. One presumes that Uncle Joe, watching the proceedings, was cheering on the billy goat.

Uncle Joe's nephew, whose yard he shared, was also named Joe. As a younger man the nephew had an alcohol habit and could get quite violent. One time Red's mom, then a teenager, was having a party. He showed up at the front door with a butcher knife, which he thrust through the screen door before departing. He was as drunk as a robin eating fermented palm berries, and he didn't like to be bothered by the noise. By the time we knew him, however, he had sobered up and was a friendly old codger.

Down the road apiece lived an older doctor and his family. His younger wife had flaming red hair, with a fiery personality to match, and was a good friend of Red's mother. She was a very talented artist, and she loved to smoke, drink, and party in general. They had a swimming pool way out back behind the house and she had a phone installed there—very unique and "progressive" for those days. She was a plant aficionado and had a large collection of orchids, many of which she brought back from numerous trips to her favorite destination, Guatemala. She loved animals too, and had quite a menagerie, including two tall standard poodles, a cuddly koala bear, and two large Amazon parrots.

Those birds were very vociferous, and had a variety of shrieks, whistles, and words in their vocabulary. They lived in large cages by the front door in front of a large picture window, with a great view of the road and the river. It was not unusual to ride a bike by their house (the doors and windows were always open), and hear someone shriek at the top of his lungs, "Hello, pretty, hello,

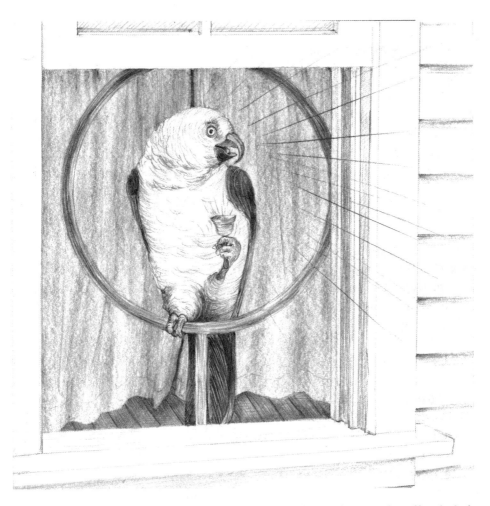

hello." Many people were quite taken aback, if not downright offended, for they didn't know it was not a lecherous man yelling and whistling at them, but the birds. And of course, every time the parrots shrieked, the dogs would start barking wildly and running around the house.

Between the birds, dogs, and kids, that house was in a constant uproar, and the lady of the house loved every cacophonous minute of it. Perhaps she was so lively because she drank copious amounts of coffee throughout the day. Once a week or so, when the cupboard was empty, she paid the kids a nickel a cup to go around the property and gather up all the missing coffee cups—they could be found in the house, at the pool, in her studio, in her car, and almost anywhere else around the yard, for she carried coffee with her everywhere.

Not being coffee drinkers ourselves, Red and I preferred Coca-Cola. One day we were riding our bikes downtown to have a Coke at "Doc" Campbell's drugstore, where we sat at the counter on those swivel-topped stools we loved to play on. Red's dad had been a soda jerk at Campbell's when he was a teenager.

Red stopped in front of an old building with large columns in front. It had once been the most ornate bank in Cocoa, but was now the office of one of the few lawyers in town, Mr. John D. Shepard. Mr. Shepard was undoubtedly one of the wealthiest men in Brevard county and one of its best known lawyers. He specialized in real estate law, and had one of the largest law libraries in the state of Florida. The old bank building was somewhat rundown, but evidence of its former glory days was everywhere: columns inside with Corinthian capitals, marble floors and counter tops, and in the back, the huge, original, bank safe. Nothing about all of this seemed so unusual, until Red pointed out what was covering the floor and table tops — everywhere were heaps and piles and stacks of papers, each with a "paperweight" on top — paperweights of every description. There were ashtrays, rocks, large bolts, cups, shells, books — almost anything would do. This was Mr. Shepard's filing system. Although it looked quite chaotic, Mr. Shepard, with a mind as sharp as a stingaree tail, knew precisely where everything was.

One day Mr. Shepard was talking to Cocoa's favorite doctor, Dr. Thomas Kenaston, Sr. Dr. Kenaston had delivered Red, removed her tonsils, and tended to three generations of her family and Red loved him — he was the old-timey family physician, for whom medicine was a calling, not a business. This particular day, Dr. Kenaston was telling his old friend, Mr. Shepard, that he ought to take some time off and spend some of his hard earned money, after all he couldn't take it with him. To which Mr. Shepard replied, "Then I won't go!" And he almost didn't — he worked up into his eighties, walking the mile or so down the river road in to work every day, usually seven days a week — and finally died in his nineties. His grandson restored the office to its original grandeur, painting the columns, polishing the marble, and adding antique furniture. Gone were the stacks and stacks of papers, and gone was another well-known fixture in Cocoa, John D. Shepard.

Merritt Island had its share of characters and funny names. We heard about most of them from Red's dad. Besides Alvah and Alvaretta, there was A Fortenberry, whose first name was just "A." He had one son named Cubic, and another son John, whom Red's dad used to pal around with. His eldest son was Gordon, who was a professional boxer for a while. A fourth brother was W.E., called Winnie. They are all buried in the old cemetery nestled in the scrub oaks on the Barge Canal on North Merritt Island, sadly now right beside the decidedly un-peaceful "Beach-Line Expressway."

West of A's sawmill, on the corner of Merritt Island Causeway and South Tropical Trail there was the post office, where the postmaster, Mr. Bracco, worked. There he had the outhouse that Red's dad and friends on Halloween used to move out into the middle of the road for fun. Next to him, there was a grocery store owned by Deforest Prine, who had a brother named Hermus, who was a builder. Red's dad said he was one of the best carpenters he had ever known. Hermus would inspect each board individually, looking down its length to see if there was any warp at all. If a board was not perfectly straight, he tossed it on the cull pile and inspected another one. Red's dad said he was such a perfectionist that if you had a house built by him, you had a very fine house indeed.

On the north side of the causeway was Norwood's, a large, frame building with polished wood floors, where all the kids used to go to skate. It also served as a dance hall. Down the road, on North Tropical Trail was Mr. Dewey's nursery, and across the street, Brabham's grocery store, run by Miss La Verne Brabham, a spinster whom everyone called Auntie Verne. This was a favorite spot of the kids, as it had a particularly good sulfur well, and they piped the water through the meat locker, so it came out ice cold. Although northerners turn their noses up at sulfur water, it really hit the spot with those kids — and everyone else — on a hot summer day.

On South Tropical Trail, around the first curve off Hwy 520, lived an older lady, Mrs. Haskell. She had many avocado trees in her yard, which Red's dad used to pick. The "old lady who lived in a shoe" had nothing on this old lady — when her frame house burned down, she moved into her chicken coop, which was about the size of a car, and there she stayed. Just down the road from her lived Harold Wilson, the surveyor, whose watermelons Red's dad and friends used to pilfer.

Mail order brides must have been popular way back then. In the early 1930's, on one corner of 520 and South Tropical Trail there was a ramshackle, dilapidated old apartment building owned by an equally ramshackle old geezer who must have been in his '70's or '80's. He sent off for a mail order bride, who arrived by train. Legend has it that when he met her at the depot, the first thing he did was to raise her skirt! He saw her drawers were dingy, and promptly sent her back north on the next train. He tried a mail-order bride a second time and presumably the next one had clean bloomers, so he kept her. She even had a child by him, but by most accounts, she was a real termagant — the shrew of the neighborhood.

Around the same time, Red's dad said the lighthouse keeper at Cape Canaveral was Mr. Harry Atkinson. He was an extremely nice man, but couldn't seem to find a wife locally. So he also put out an ad for a mail-order bride and luckily ended up with a woman as nice as he was. They had no children of their own and were both very fond of Red's dad and his younger brothers and often invited them out to stay at the lighthouse. While there, they would go hunting for rabbits. Mr. Atkinson would drive the car at night along the rutted, sandy beach roads, winding through the palmetto scrub while Red's dad rode on the front fender with a shotgun. When a rabbit came into view of the headlights, it would stop, temporarily blinded by the lights, and Red's dad would shoot it. Mrs. Atkinson was a good cook and cooked all kinds of wild game besides rabbit, including raccoon.

The Atkinsons had a pet cat they called Jingle Balls. At some point they decided to castrate this cat, which was accomplished somehow—there were no such things as veterinarians back then. Anyhow, the boys were out visiting one day, and Mr. Atkinson was calling the cat to come eat, "Here Jingle Balls, here boy." Red's uncle, about five years old at the time piped up and said, "He's just Jingle now, Mr. Atkinson."

In 1938, Mr. Atkinson was transferred to the Jupiter lighthouse, and that year invited Red's dad and brother to spend the summer with them, an opportunity they jumped at with great joy. At Jupiter Inlet, the Atlantic Ocean, the Loxahatchee River and the Indian River all met in a glorious, clear water, grass-covered bottom, estuarine tidal basin. Because of this, the fishing at Jupiter was fantastic and they had the place all to themselves because very few people lived there. One day Red's dad went fishing with a local boy in his small rowboat. The tide was in and the water crystal clear. They spotted a huge snook nearby and paddled right up to it. It was as long as their boat. The other boy thrust his spear into the monster and it promptly swam under the boat, breaking the wooden spear handle. The rope, however, was tied to the metal spear head itself, and the boys held on for dear life. That huge fish pulled them and the boat all around the inlet before they finally landed it. They took it to the fish market, where it weighed in at forty-two pounds. They sold it for a nickel a pound.

It was truly a wild Florida then—the town of Jupiter was practically nonexistent. That year, 1938, Jupiter High School graduated four students—three girls and a boy. That was one of the best summers of Red's dad's life. Little did he know that in just a few short years he would be going off to fight in WWII, and Florida as he knew it would soon change forever.

14—Red's Theory of Relativity

Red's family was rather eccentric. "Shrimpette," she explained one day, "when some average work-a-day person is a little nutty, people call him just that—nutty, crazy, loco, or looney. But if you are wealthy and a little 'off,' people call you eccentric. There's really no difference."

She knew she had some lulus in her family.

There was Aunt Loretta. Tall and thin like all of Red's mother's family, she had hands like a child's, untouched by time. No wrinkles, no age spots, no callouses. Red explained that was because they were also untouched by dish water, garden dirt, or diapers. Aunt Loretta was the last of a dying breed of aristocratic, imperious, old women who lived and died like queens. She was an anachronism even in the 1970's. Late in her life, she just took to her bed and never got up—for several years—until she died. No one knew of anything particularly *wrong* with her, she was just old and tired and stayed in bed, with round-the-clock maids to wait on her hand and foot.

Aunt Loretta had no children of her own, so she made it her business to give advice on raising first her niece, Red's mom (who had been motherless since the age of five), then on rearing Red and her brother. When dining with Aunt Loretta, you always had to eat your vegetables. Bad manners were not tolerated, nor was what she considered to be bad cooking. It was common for her to go into the kitchen of even the best restaurants to give the chef some advice on how to cook a particular dish. The fact that she had never cooked, having servants to do it, never stopped her from telling someone else how. Of course, down here in the South, she never thought the cooks knew what they were doing.

Aunt Loretta had a whole floor of a ritzy Park Avenue apartment building as her home. She had box seats at the Metropolitan Opera, shopped on Fifth Avenue, and she spent part of the winter in Florida.

In 1975, Aunt Loretta about died of apoplexy. It seems that a utilities company in which she was heavily invested, Con Edison, cut their dividend to shareholders. Aunt Loretta was sure that another depression was coming and that year her nieces and nephews received no Christmas presents: she had to save her money for the coming crash. In the '70's, she loathed Red's straight, long hair, and would send her mother pictures from magazines of "suitable hair-dos" for her great-niece. Red told me that one time when she visited Aunt Loretta in New York City, they went to lunch at a swanky restaurant. On the way, she had her chauffeur stop at a store, where she bought Red some hair clips for her to wear while dining.

As a dyed-in-the-wool Yankee, Aunt Loretta did not think much of Southern cooking and was appalled when Red's family would eat fried chicken with their fingers. She liked her vegetables lightly steamed and *nothing* fried. Like her brother Uncle Fritz, who would sometimes emphatically order "only five french fries" with his burger, she ate very abstemiously. In fact, all that family had strange eating habits. Red's mother also ate very sparingly and she ate the exact same thing for breakfast and lunch every day—oatmeal and toast for breakfast and for lunch tomato, onion and avocado, with another piece of toast. When her own avocado trees were done producing for the season, she would buy avocadoes at the store, even though they were imported and inferior, so addicted was she to them. This seemed to be her one extravagance. Every single day, day in, day out, year in, year out, she ate the same thing!

Red's brother also had the same habit as an adult—one egg and a piece of bacon for breakfast, and a bologna sandwich, potato chips and Coke for lunch. Every day, always the same, *ad infinitum,* or perhaps, *ad nauseum.* And he never ate fruit or vegetables, which drove Red's mom to distraction. "Duncan," she would say, "you're going to die of scurvy or beri-beri one day."

Duncan would bring his friends from college home over their vacations. Red often surprised them by whipping up waffles or pancakes for breakfast—not that that was such a surprise—but it was the color of them. She would make them an eye-popping shade of red, green, or blue, using food coloring, probably making them gag if they happened to have a hangover that morning. Those guys likely never forgot her colorful cuisine.

Unfortunately for Red's dad, Red's mom cooked like her Yankee relatives. Although she never lived in the north, she still cooked that way, proving, as Red's dad said, "genetics is much more important than habitat." Red's dad liked southern cooking—fried chicken, fried okra, and anything, such as field peas or green beans, cooked all day with ham hock. He always felt deprived because his wife did not like to cook that way.

Uncle Fritz, Aunt Loretta's brother, was Red's favorite great-uncle. He never had a real job, not having to work, and so he and his wife spent long winters in Florida, on our River Road. They were in the class of the idle rich—fairly rich, and extremely idle. Fritzi-Ritz, as Red called him, was a grand tennis player, and in the early twentieth century, he played with all the "greats," such as Don Budge and Maurice McLoughlin, the "California Comet." In fact, Red's grandmother, Fritz's sister, also was a nationally ranked tennis player, and was rumored to almost have married Mr. McLoughlin.

Another of Uncle Fritz's athletic claims to fame was his prowess with a fly swatter. He would brag that he could kill a fly sitting on whipped cream without disturbing the whipped cream, and actually demonstrated it successfully many times.

Uncle Fritz also had an anatomical curiousity—the index finger on his right hand was cut off at the first knuckle—the result of a testy chain on an

old Indian motorbike he was fooling with when he was a boy. In spite of the loss, his tennis playing seemed to be unimpaired, and he was a first-class golfer as well.

In later years, Red would say, "Can you imagine that happening to someone today — some lawyer would be right there, wanting to sue the motorcycle manufacturer. But in those days, I'm sure his parents scolded him for being a very careless boy, which he was, and that was that.

"You see," she continued, "back in those days, people understood about taking responsibility for their actions. If a kid jumped off your dock and broke his leg, it was his fault, not yours for having the dock. If a kid trespassed on your property and got kicked by your horse, it was his fault, not yours, as it is now, for having an 'attractive nuisance.'"

"This is one reason that we have so many laws now, protecting everyone — no one will take responsibility for doing dumb things. The end result has been a gradual but drastic loss of our freedoms. Now you need a license or a permit to do almost anything — to use a boat, to build a porch, to dig a pond, to build a dock, it never ends.

"There's a law requiring helmets for motorcycles and bicycles, and some cities even require a bicycle license! There are required permits for car ownership, boat ownership, even dog ownership, which all cost us money. One must have a license to fish and to hunt. We are being licensed and permitted — which are just really other names for taxes — into the poor house, and our government still operates in a deficit. Thomas Jefferson said it best, 'That government is best which governs least.'"

Red ranted on, "Not only that, but attending to these endless bureaucratic paper trails robs us of our free time! Life has become way too complicated."

She was still on her soap box.

"One by one our freedoms get taken away and people don't even realize it. But the bottom line is that people don't realize that freedom and responsibility go hand in hand. You cannot have freedom without responsibility. Why, I even think that someday freedom of the press will be taken away because the media are so irresponsible. And it would serve them right. The real bottom line is there are too many people now, and too many who aren't taught to be responsible for their own actions. And as a result, toes get stepped on, necessitating endless rules, regulations, and laws. In the old days, if someone did something irresponsible, he usually paid the price for it, either with inconvenience or injury to himself, or by being shamed and shunned by society."

Red sighed.

"Okay," she said, "I'll get off my soapbox now, Shrimpette. I just wish I could have lived back in Uncle Fritz's day. Life was so much simpler then."

Uncle Fritz was a teetotaler, a non-smoker, a strict, conservative Republican, and a devout Catholic. Unfortunately, he married a beautiful woman with more pedigree than wealth, who smoked, drank martinis, was a very liberal Democrat, and never would convert to Catholicism. He married her for her looks, and she married him for his money—a marriage not exactly made in Heaven. They stayed married all their lives—his strict Catholicism made divorce unthinkable—but it was a loveless marriage, only made bearable by their constant whirlwind of parties and entertaining.

Fritz always drove the car, and he drove like a maniac. Red guessed that was why Edna always rode in the back seat of the big station wagon, letting Fritz chauffeur her around—it was safer back there. Years later, Red's mom did the same thing, always riding in the back seat while Red's dad drove her around. She claimed it was because of her bad back. Maybe it was just one of those familial foibles, learned from Aunt Edna.

Uncle Fritz was very taken with famous people and loved to drop names. At their estate in New Jersey, they entertained lavishly, often having the governor, famous tennis players, movie starlets, and Mr. Lenox, founder of Lenox China, to dinner. At their famous Sunday night dinners, they would always show first-run Twentieth Century Fox films after dinner in the huge, oak-paneled dining room. The room was so large that a regular size movie screen was at one end of the room, covered by a curtain. The family had connections with Fox Films, and Fritz had all the big stars' photos—all autographed—on the walls of his projection room, which was at the other end of the dining room. On the mantel of the fireplace of this great room sat a priceless porcelain Tiffany clock and two matching candelabra. Guests always ate on Lenox china, some of it "Special Editions," patterns made just for their family. The story went that after Mr. Lenox died, he left the company to someone in Fritz's family, because they had given him the money to start his porcelain factory when he was but a penniless Irish immigrant with nothing but a dream. Thereafter, anyone in Red's family who got married received a barrel of china in the pattern of their choice for a wedding present. Consequently, Red's house was chock-full of the beautiful stuff, not only her grandmother's pattern, but many other tea sets, breakfast sets, and odd pieces.

When in Florida, during the early days of the space program, Uncle Fritz loved meeting the astronauts, who were practically looked upon as gods back then. At that time, Red was a young teenager, and she remembered they all drove Corvettes. On weekend nights, they would park them in a row outside their favorite hangouts—the Mousetrap Lounge or Lee Caron's Carnival Club at Cocoa Beach. One time a friend who worked for NASA brought the astronaut Wally Schirra around to Red's house and he autographed a picture for her. Red recalled that he was a very jovial, extroverted, and nice man.

Uncle Fritz and Aunt Loretta's father, who was Red's great grandfather, was a wealthy landowner in New York and New Jersey. In 1884 he married an equally wealthy daughter of a German brewery owner and together they produced ten children. Red's grandmother was one of them. They spent the winter in New York City, and when school was out, would load all ten children, their dogs, ponies, and trunks and trunks of clothing onto a private train, and move to their summer home, a Victorian mansion on a large farm in New Jersey. Red said the house had nine bedrooms, several fireplaces, spacious porches and a huge kitchen, with a tremendous woodburning stove for cooking. The downstairs rooms were all paneled in oak, hand carved by German artisans. The builder of this house, Red's great grandfather, was the same man who was so fond of poker that he had three identical card tables made for his various houses, including one for Red's house in Florida, where he visited regularly.

In the 1920's, he and his wife would make the trip from up north in their chauffeur driven car down to see their daughter, Red's grandmother, in our town. They also owned some orange groves in the area. Once in Florida, it was an endless round of winter parties, soirees, and tea parties for the mother, her daughter, and granddaughter (Red's mother—then a young child). Together with other society doyennes and their daughters, such as the Parrishes and the Shepards, they would take the chauffeur driven car (quite a sight in our little town) to take tea at one of two local teahouses.

One was a stucco house on the river in Bellwood, which doubled as a millinery shop, for the proprietress also sold beautiful hats. The other was Christine's, on the river near Eau Gallie, where the specialty was gingerbread topped with whipped cream. There they would eat dainties and sip tea, or hot chocolate, dressed in long dresses, gloves, and elegant hats.

Red's mom "escaped" this kind of life as an adult because her mother died when she was five. Then her mother's family's influence became much less, and she was left to be brought up in the wilds of the orange groves and river—I once heard her mother say she was a rough-and-tumble tomboy child. Her great-grandmother must have been spinning in her grave to have her progeny brought up in so undignified a manner. If her mother had lived, she would most assuredly have been sent to boarding school in Europe and finishing schools up north.

"My goodness," Red's mom said, "can you imagine me in a finishing school? I would have been kicked out the first week. They would have never made a society belle out of me!"

As a result of her lack of "proper" rearing and because she would never move up north to be near her family, Red's mom became the black sheep of the family, which suited her just fine. She didn't much care for her Yankee relatives anyway.

Red's mom was a wonderful, intelligent woman, but true to her family's genes, became more eccentric the older she got. Although she attended a very prestigious southern university and majored in chemistry, something women of her era didn't much do, (only two girls out of her high school class of twenty three even went to college), she never quite got the hang of language. Her family dubbed her "Mrs. Malaprop," for her use—or mis-use—of words was well known in her family circle.

One time, while out fishing, she saw a sailboat with a lovely, carved wooden figurehead on its bow. "Isn't that a beautiful maidenhead," she exclaimed, while her husband laughed out loud.

When they returned to land after being on rough water, she proclaimed, "It's nice to be back on *terra cotta,* instead of *terra firma.*"

Her word pronunciation was equally haphazard. The herb oregano came out like the state Oregon-o, and mesquite was pronounced mess-quite. She was also known for calling any place that washed things, be it a car wash or a laundry, a "washateria," pronounced like cafeteria. She didn't mind her family laughing at her mispronunciations and malapropisms, and always said, "It's better to make people laugh than cry."

It seemed the older she got, the shabbier the clothes Red's mom wore around the house. One day while hanging out clothes with her mother, Red exclaimed, "Mom, these are the most tattered clothes I've ever seen. The elastic is all gone, and this T-shirt is so threadbare, you could read a paper through it! These pants are held together by a safety pin and these towels are so thin, they only have one side. Someday, you will be one of those old people they write about in the newspaper—'Old woman found in rags, ate nothing but fruit from her yard her last years. Had thousands in the bank!' Don't you know if your mother weren't already dead, she would die to see you wearing these rags."

Her mom just shrugged and said, "But these clothes are so comfortable and they're just getting broken in. And I don't wear them out in public. Besides, all the money I save on clothes you will inherit some day."

Red just sighed and gave up. Eventually she would slip the threadbare towels into the ragbag when her mother wasn't looking. Of course, Red was not exactly a fashion plate herself. She insisted on dressing for comfort—casual shorts or jeans, tennis shoes in the winter and barefoot in the summer. Her yard-work clothes were usually tattered, holey shirts (air-conditioned, she called them), and shorts, and a variety of funny hats to keep the sun off.

Red's father's family were not quite so eccentric, but some of them were rather different. They were long-time Melbourne, Florida, residents, some of them owning most of the town at one time. Red's grandfather on her father's side had been very unusual for his day and time: He had been a student of the occult, Oriental religions, the teachings of Madame Blavatsky and Rudolf Steiner, and did a stint on a bio-dynamic, organic farm in New York state. This was in the early part of the 1900's, long before Red's parents even knew each other. Much later, these things were swept into vogue again with the "hippie" movement.

Red's dad also had a cousin who was a professional whistler. She had an all-woman band that toured the country, and she whistled for a living back in the 1920's.

Red's father came from a genetically long-lived line. Her grandfather, the occultist, lived to almost one hundred. His father, Red's great grandfather, was a retired physician in Melbourne. He died in his nineties of skin cancer. He could easily have cured it when it first started, but he was old and ready to go. Another cousin, the whistler, lived to be ninety-seven.

Her physician great grandfather had owned most of what is now west Melbourne in the 1920's. He bought the property because he believed that it had oil underground. His company actually drilled for oil near Turkey Creek and found some. However, it was not enough to bother with, and eventually the land was sold for taxes.

Between her parents' families, Red had some pretty entertaining and eccentric kinfolk—as Red would say, "sanity or insanity, it's all relative."

15—In Red's Garden

At heart, Red was a farmer. She loved the land and she loved making it produce. In fact, one day she told me that by using one of her "theories," you could have predicted she would be a farmer. I was dubious, but all ears.

"Shrimpette," she said, "I have this theory that the kind of car in which you come home from the hospital when you are born will determine your future path in life. Take my family, for example. My brother came home from the hospital in a Cadillac convertible. Today, he is inclined to the socialite life—associating with the elite, living in a fancy neighborhood, and driving an expensive car are important to him. On the other hand, when I was born, I came home from the hospital in a pick-up truck, and all I ever wanted was to drive a truck and be a farmer!" She smiled triumphantly, her point was proven.

Whether flowers or edibles, Red grew it all. She had many gorgeous flower beds and always told people she'd rather get her flowers now, thank you, than wait till she was dead and couldn't enjoy them. And she figured if she had no one to give her flowers, she would grow them for herself.

Red explained to me that this part of Florida is considered subtropical, but due to the topography, parts of the area are downright tropical. Because it is surrounded by two rivers, Merritt Island can grow much more cold-tender vegetation than can the mainland. Not so long ago—fifty years or so—there was a great deal of farming in the area and many different kinds of fruits and produce were grown.

Great groves of avocadoes, mangoes and guavas used to dominate Merritt Island, and at one time it even boasted several pineapple plantations. Red bragged that the best guava jelly in the world was produced in a factory locally.

When Red's dad was a kid during the Depression, a rather odd fellow had a great big watermelon patch near their home on Merritt Island. This man seldom spoke and never smiled. He grew beautiful, succulent watermelons, and a group of boys would sneak in and swipe a ripe melon every so often. After all, food was scarce, and it was so steamy hot in the summer, those juicy, red watermelons were a temptation no boy could resist. One day, the watermelon farmer, Mr. Wilson, took them by surprise as they were busy choosing and helping themselves to yet another sweet, luscious treat from his garden.

"Boys," he drawled, "boys, from now on...." It seemed that hours were passing as he slowly delivered what they thought would be a well-deserved scolding—or maybe he was going to call the sheriff. Beads of sweat rolled down their faces, and they hardly dared to look at him. "Boys, from now on, you will take your watermelons all from the row nearest the road, and not from all over the patch." The boys heaved a huge sigh of relief and broke out grinning, "Thank you, Mr. Wilson, thank you. We'll do just as you say." The enthusiasm was infectious, as he was smiling too. This was about the extent of thievery in those days.

That same group of boys on Halloween used to play a prank on another Merritt Island neighbor. Mr. Bracco was the postmaster at the post office on the corner of South Tropical Trail and Merritt Island Causeway, and behind the post office he had a one-seater outhouse. Late on Halloween night the boys would hoist it up on two-by-fours and tote it into the middle of the intersection and leave it there. Fortunately, there was no traffic to speak of, so no harm came to it, but Mr. Bracco was probably surprised when he came out in the morning to find it gone.

In those days, the 1920's and '30's, when Red's dad was a lad and living in Merritt Park, one of his neighbors was Dave Nisbet. Mr. Nisbet, among other things, grew sour orange root stock for citrus grafting. He paid Red's dad a nickel a quart for the seeds which he had to squeeze laboriously from of a big pile of sour oranges. A nickel doesn't sound like much now, Red said, but in those days it would buy an ice cream cone, a movie show, or one shot-gun shell.

Some beautiful specimens of the *gumbo limbo* tree exist on Merritt Island, which is the northernmost end of their range. Of course, citrus thrives there also, as on the mainland. But the tenderer varieties such as key limes and lemons do much better on the Island, as do the tasty, succulent mangoes. Red pointed out that bananas grow well everywhere in these parts, as do bromeliads and other epiphytes, including a dainty native orchid, *encyclia*, found mostly in the large, graceful oak trees seen hereabouts.

Red was disgusted with the way people had come to Florida and planted just anything without considering the consequences to the native environment.

"There have been three major pestiferous introduced species of plants, and scores of minor ones, that have all but taken over parts of south Florida: the *melaleuca,* or punk tree, the Brazilian pepper tree, and the Australian pine. Only the latter has some redeeming value, but not enough to outweigh its disadvantages.

"The Australian pine was brought in and planted on dikes surrounding citrus groves as effective windbreaks. They are effective enough, but they are rather cold-tender and they spread like crazy, crowding out native species. Now that great stands of them have been frozen, the dead wood must be gotten rid of, and it turns out that in spite of being a pine, the wood is quite hard and good for burning."

Red continued to expound on the disastrous effects of another unwanted alien plant, the melaleuca. "This tree is a real menace in South Florida, and it's spreading north. It sucks the moisture out of the ground, stealing water from the native trees. And apiarists hate it too. They say it ruins honey. Honey from melaleuca is very thin and watery, and ferments very quickly—a fifty-five gallon drum of the stuff will ferment and blow the lid off in a matter of days. The Brazilian pepper bush is another non-native interloper that Floridians wish would go away. In South Florida, it has caused widespread devastation by crowding out native flora. Here in East Central Florida, it has really crowded out the mangroves which are so vital to our Indian River habitat."

Red had beehives in her grove, although she didn't work them herself—she lacked the patience. When newcomers started moving closer, they complained of the bees and she had to move them. "Shrimpette," she complained one day, "my family has been on this piece of land for eighty years, and now new neighbors are telling us how to live. It's not right, but there's nothing we can do about it. Of course, the Indians could say the same thing—it's not right that their native land was taken over by us, but there's not much they can do about it. In our society 'might makes right,' and these days it seems that money equals might. It's too bad."

My brother used to mow Red's yard, but she never allowed him to mow the part around the house, preferring to do it herself. It was good exercise, she proclaimed, and she didn't want him mowing down any of her precious flowers. To this day, the redolence of camphor brings back vivid memories of Red mowing her front yard, as she had a wonderful, large, shady cam-

93

phor tree there: as she mowed under it, the pungent aroma from the cut-up leaves scented the air like Grandma's room when she had a cold.

Red loved having cut flowers in the house and to this end, she would have the most gorgeous beds of zinnias all summer long. She also loved the hibiscus, even though it needed to be pruned to the ground if a freeze came along. Her property had at least one of almost every kind of fruit tree that grows in the area: avocados, bananas, persimmons, key limes, lemons, grapes, lychee nuts, mangoes, loquats, mulberries and a whole grove full of every kind of orange and grapefruit tree. And it seemed Red's mother knew every one of those citrus trees personally. After all, her father had planted most of them.

"This is a Valencia tree with a navel grafted onto it. When I was a girl, my father knew how much I liked navel oranges, and made half this tree a navel just for me," Red's mom noted as we walked through the grove one day. She picked one to show us its "belly button," as if we were Yankees and didn't know how the navel orange got its name.

"And this tree, a pineapple orange, has always had the best juice oranges," Red's mom continued. "This Duncan grapefruit was grafted onto a lemon and has never been too good, but this one was grafted onto sour root stock, and is a wonderful specimen," she said, pointing to her favorite grapefruit. "In fact, this tree is so large that when I was a kid, I used to surreptitiously climb out of my upstairs bedroom window when I was supposed to be napping. Then I'd use its huge branches to lower myself to the ground. My poor father—I was a pretty sneaky kid, I guess."

Red's yard had a long, coquina rock wall garden built by her grandfather. In it her mother would grow flowers and such, but I will always remember it for the huge Wisteria growing there. In early April, before it put on leaves, it would be covered with sweet-smelling purple blooms, hanging down in great clusters. It had branches as big around as a person's arm because it was so old. Her grandfather had planted it, and Red tended to it very carefully—it was a family heirloom as precious to her as the Lenox china.

Red's giant mulberry tree was very old and had great, sweeping branches hanging down to the ground, which then rooted, creating new trees around the periphery of the old one. In the spring when the berries were ripe, the tree would be descended upon by flocks of birds. Red always awaited the arrival of the little cedar waxwings, very beautifully colored birds which loved the mulberries. The tree would also be raided by all the neighborhood kids, sitting in its comfortable branches, stuffing the squishy berries into their mouths, and going home with purple-stained clothes and mouths. That was a wonderful old tree, as even on the hottest summer day, it was cool in the dense shade of the giant mulberry.

In the late summer and fall the first job of the day was to look for fallen avocados. Actually, Red and her mom checked all through the day for them, for if they lay on the ground too long, the squirrels would eat them. It was always a race to see who could get to the avocados first: Red or the dogs. Most of her dogs loved avocados and if they got one, were reluctant to give it up. There were always plenty for the dogs to eat—Red fed them the pears that were too gnawed on by squirrels to be edible by humans.

There were several avocado trees on her property, all of different varieties. Her mother's favorite tree was a huge, very old specimen—easily fifty feet tall. In fact, all the older avocado trees were huge—seen from across the river, they were the trees that towered above the rest. Her mother's favorite tree had pears that were bright green, very shiny, and as large as a cantaloupe, only slightly more oval than round. Another tree had very long, tear-drop shaped pears as big as a football. These particular ones were dark green with a rough skin.

Red grabbed one from a basket and said, "Doesn't this look just like 'gator hide? That's why we call them alligator pears."

One avocado tree had several large branches that hung over a tin-roofed shed in Red's yard. This tree had huge pears and during the season they would regularly fall from thirty or forty feet down onto the tin roof. Ka-pow! they would hit and sound like a gun shot. Day and night they would hit that roof, making huge dents in it. It was a credit to the older, sturdier tin that it had withstood that kind of punishment for more than fifty years.

We were investigating this old shed one day and found some old bottles, tools, and rusty nails. With a faraway look in her eyes, Red muttered, *sotto voce*, "I never knew my grandfather, but it is a nice image I have of him in this little house—it was his workshop, and I can just see him doing his beautiful carved woodwork out here in the shade of the giant avocado tree."

Sometimes in the evening, when the sun went to bed early because of thunderstorms or clouds in the west, the sky and river were identical shades of misty grey and the horizon disappeared, as water and air melted together as one. We would walk across the road to Red's avocado stand which had a sign that read, "AVOCADOS 25 cents KEY LIMES 10 cents/dozen." At the end of the day we had to check to see if any had been sold. When her old tree had a bumper crop, business boomed. People from as far

away as Orlando would come to get those particular pears, so popular and sought-after were they.

Actually, before Red, her brother Duncan had also sold avocados. In addition to his own, he would sell the neighbor lady's pears, for ten cents each. He would split the take with her: a nickel for him, a nickel for her. While Red was an entrepreneur and the family saver, Duncan also was a salesman and a wheeler-dealer. He would regularly come home with some "treasure" that he had traded some trinket to another kid for, usually coming out with the better deal. He would also bring home stuff from people's trash piles, one time dragging home a mattress for their dog Shadow to sleep on. Duncan truly lived by the motto, "one man's trash is another man's treasure."

Duncan also wheedled shopkeepers out of "good stuff" when he could. One time he was up in the ancient, musty attic of Travis Hardware Store in downtown Cocoa. A local fixture for a hundred years, you could find any hardware item there, no matter how obscure. Duncan spotted a huge piece of machinery that was collecting dust. Not even knowing for sure what it was, he offered them twenty five dollars for it, which they accepted. It turned out to be a pipe cutter and threader, weighing about two hundred pounds—a very good piece of machinery. Somehow he got it home, where it was used regularly, there always being much pipe repair work to be done around the property, and this was long before PVC was used.

But Duncan was not the only one who foraged for bounty on our river road.

There were many varmints that preyed upon the various fruits in our yards. In Red's yard, the squirrels made sure no humans ever found a pecan, they also wiped out the peach crops, and ate big holes in the avocados and mangoes. What made Red's mom so mad was that they would not eat a whole avocado; they had to sample several, leaving holes in lots of them. They would even eat them while the pear was still hanging on the tree. Squirrels would also eat oranges if there was nothing else.

The 'coons fairly decimated the mangoes, the sweet corn, the persimmons, and worst of all, Red's dad's precious grapes. Those raccoons would clean off a grape vine overnight, very daintily peeling the grapes and leaving their tell-tale sign of grape husks all over the ground. 'Coons also loved the little bananas. Other critters such as 'possums and birds ate the figs, the tomatoes, and the guavas.

Of course, the chickens did their share of damage also. They loved to eat the ripe, red tomatoes hanging on the vines. And when Red had baby orphan chicks to raise, she would let the tomato-eating caterpillars grow on them in order to feed them to the baby chicks. They went crazy for those caterpillars. Red's mom would fume, "I can't believe you're sacrificing those good tomatoes for those chickens! It's bad enough that the big chickens peck holes in the tomatoes, but now you're raising caterpillars on them for those biddies!" Red said she had to plant two of everything: one for the animals and one for her family.

Red's parents grew a couple of red and pink grapefruit trees just for friends, as they preferred for themselves the old variety of seedy, white grapefruit called Duncan. These were the largest, juiciest, most flavorful grapefruit ever grown. Red explained that when one starts hybridizing for traits such as seedlessness (demanded as more convenient these days by housewives), and color, other traits are lost, such as size and flavor. She used the grapefruit as an example of what our society was becoming: people were preferring looks and convenience over substance and taste.

"Any old-time citrus grower will tell you the older, plainer-looking varieties have the best flavor. And any citrus grower will also tell you the fruit grown in the center of the state (not to mention California) tastes like water compared with that of citrus from the Indian River area."

Red's family used to send fruit to friends and relatives at Christmas. As a joke, they would throw in a calamondin, a tiny, sour fruit that looks like a miniature orange, and label it "California Orange." They would also put in a ponderosa lemon, which looked like a grapefruit, and label it "California Grapefruit."

During World War II and just after, there was a branch of the federal bureaucracy called the OPA, the Office of Price Administration. It would weekly set prices on all food items, so that no shop-keeper could gouge. In Wilmington, Delaware, where Red's dad was living at the time, he said that in the fruit department of the grocery stores, the citrus would be separated. One bin for Indian River citrus, and one bin for all the rest—the fruit from the Indian River earned a higher OPA price.

Red wasn't sure why the citrus on the Indian River was the best, but she thought perhaps it was something to do with the coquina rock supplying minerals, plus the fact that the sand and coquina allowed water to drain through the soil—citrus trees not liking "wet feet." All the groves in the vicinity of the Indian River were sitting on coquina rock.

Coquina is a very soft, porous rock, made primarily of seashells. It breaks apart rather easily, but it sure made early grove planting pioneers work for their money. Red's mom remembered in the early days of citrus farming,

when the groves were first being put in, the constant sound of dynamite booms in the distance. A hole had to be blown in the coquina for every tree to be planted. She explained that trees planted on top of the rock would never thrive or get large—they would just kind of sit there, becoming little bonzai fruit trees.

Curiously, the coquina rock on the river bank had numerous, large, perfectly round holes in it. When I wondered what could produce a hole so perfectly round in the rock, Red explained, "They were caused by trees that were growing when the rock was formed millions of years ago. As the trees died, the round holes were left in the rock where the root ball had been."

Besides fruit trees, Red's yard had many nice palm trees, mostly the native sabal palm, called "cabbage palm" by locals. Most newcomers regarded them almost as trash trees and developers cut them down by the thousands. Red despised this practice.

"Each of these palms is a mini-ecosystem by itself," she said, indignantly. "People don't realize that in the crown of the tree, among the palm fronds at the top live a myriad of critters. Of course most people consider these critters repugnant and pestiferous. However, those roaches, rats, and snakes that live up there serve a vital function in our ecosystem: they are near the bottom of the food chain, and as such, are prey for more 'desirable' species, such as hawks and owls. Not only that, but many birds eat the cabbage palm berries, guinea wasps build nests under the protective fronds, birds nest in them, and the *Heliconia* butterflies roost in their fronds at night. Most people don't even realize the age of these palms. They are extremely slow growing, and one that is only twenty feet tall is about thirty to forty years old. Some of the tall ones are easily fifty to one hundred years old."

Whenever a cabbage palm was cut down in the neighborhood, Red's mom would always send someone over to harvest the tender "heart of palm" for her to eat. In the late fall, when the robins arrived, the cabbage palm berries were in great abundance. The Robins loved them, and often ate so many fermented berries that they would get very drunk, wobbling around and unable to fly. Red's yard also used to have some of the most beautiful palms of all — the royal palm. Too tender, they all eventually succumbed to freezing temperatures. But some still remain on Merritt Island, and Red once told me about the road by Thomas Alva Edison's house in Fort Myers, lined with stately royal palms that Mr. Edison planted there.

Red compared man with trees: those that could bend in a storm without breaking, such as the palms and bamboo, would survive whole; those that were rigid and inflexible would lose limbs or be uprooted. It was important, therefore, to be flexible and to bend with the winds of change, she said. I believe Red used her time weeding and watering her garden to contemplate these and other truths and mysteries of the world, as William Blake wrote,

> ...to see a World in a Grain of Sand
> And a Heaven in a Wild Flower
> Hold Infinity in the palm of your hand
> And eternity in an hour.

Inasmuch as Red could see the hand of God in all things animate and inanimate, she could see the supernatural in all of nature. As part of her animistic tendencies, and in spite of being a scientist herself, she abhorred the way modern science was bent on removing all traces of a "soul" from nature. She agreed with Poe, in his *Sonnet: To Science* when he wrote:

> ...Hast thou (science) not torn
> the Naiad from her flood,
> The Elfin from the green grass, and from me
> The summer dream beneath the tamarind tree?

Red worked tirelessly in her gardens, and you never knew what she would be into next. At one point, she decided to build a garden to attract butterflies. She got every book on *lepidoptera* and read up on what they liked to eat and what they liked to lay their eggs on. Of course, she had to learn which species inhabited this part of the world, and also all about their life cycle. To this end, she built some small butterfly cages, where she could bring in the larvae, or caterpillars, and feed them until they made cocoons. Then, after a period of time, they would emerge as beautiful, adult butterflies.

"Could anything be more magical and marvelous than the metamorphasis of caterpillars to cocoons to butterflies? Surely this alone could convince even the most hardened atheist of the presence of God's hand in nature," she would say.

She took great pains to attract the monarch butterfly by planting milkweed. Once they laid their eggs, she would snip the branch and bring it inside. There she would keep it fed with fresh milkweed sprigs until it grew large enough to change into a *chrysalis*—arguably the most beautiful of all lepidoptera pupae. A monarch chrysalis (from the Greek word for gold, she explained), is a delicate green with gold dots. Over a period of about two weeks, the black and white wings of the adult butterfly could be seen through the thin, transluscent green skin of the chrysalis, until one day, this membrane would break, and out would emerge the adult monarch, wings folded up. It would sit for a few hours, drying and spreading its wings, until it was able to fly off, ready to feed and start the process all over again by laying eggs on another milkweed plant.

Red would always let me release the butterflies, and with a lump in my throat I would watch them fly away.

Then she built a large arbor to grow vines on. She had the passion vine, which provided food for the caterpillar of the fritillary and zebra long-wing butterflies. The passion vine had the most delicate and intricate flowers, and the fruits were edible and quite tasty. There was also the curiously beautiful Dutchman's pipe vine, food for the Polydamus swallowtail caterpillar. She planted dill and fennel for the black swallowtail to lay its eggs on, their larvae being her favorite—beautiful green and black striped caterpillars with bright yellow dots.

One summer she and a friend built a pond, hacking through the coquina to make it deep enough. Around it she planted milkweed for the monarch butterflies, as well as numerous kinds of bromeliads, including several dozen pineapples, which would produce in the summer.

Now, there is hardly anything tastier than a homegrown pineapple. As Red would say, they are one of many things in the garden that teach the gardener patience; a pineapple takes two to three years to produce a flower, or "inflorescence," which is beautiful in itself—brilliant pink and purple. From this, it takes another three to four months to ripen to an edible fruit. But what a joy to cut one and sink your teeth into it, the sweet, nectar-like juice running down your chin!

In her pond she had beautiful koi, fantails, and other goldfish. More than once we waded in ditches looking for crawdads. She said they were a favorite food for the big bullfrogs she had collected and which thrived in her pond. There were numerous southern leopard frogs also, and any water turtle she found she would put in there. It was a wonderful little water habitat, and beautiful too, with several different kinds of water lilies and other blooming swamp plants which Red gathered from marshy wetlands. She was not afraid to wade in boggy swamps or weedy ditches in search of her flora and fauna, it was always just another adventure.

While working in her garden, Red constantly opined to anyone who was there. "Think before you plant: what do you want this garden to look like in five years, ten, twenty—ultimately? Visualize how you want it to look. Be careful before you plant invasive, easily diseased, too demanding plants. Be prepared to take care of them until they are the 'ultimate' garden, and after that too. Plan the life of your garden—from before the first seed till... well, forever! Be patient and open to growth—the life of a garden is like a creature—it is not a static thing, but ever changing and growing."

Another of Red's famous theories was that you could tell a lot about people by looking at their gardens. Did they keep them well weeded? Did they plant with some kind of plan in mind, or just stick plants in willy-nilly? Were their gardens neat, well trimmed, and manicured, or over-grown, wild, and jungle-like? Did people use just green shrubbery, or did they use color? She said she could tell if people were neat or sloppy, organized or haphazard, boring or exciting, by observing their gardens.

Red's gardens exemplified her free-spirit nature and her desire that flower gardens should be "a riot of color." She believed that in nature there was no color combination that was unacceptable. Purples, oranges, reds, blues and yellows, she threw them in all together. Her flower gardens were a sensuous treat for the eyes; everywhere you looked in her yard there was color. Her garden was at once disheveled madness with an underlying order, chaos with a method to it which only she knew, colorful, yet contained; and one supposes, according to her "theory," so was her life.

But most of all, her garden was a place of peace and quiet, and she was happy to share it with her friends and their dogs. All the dogs loved it back there, and her dog Polly was her constant companion while she was building these gardens. After Polly was gone, Red's dad put an engraved marble stone for her in the garden. She wasn't really buried there, as Red kept her ashes in her room, but Polly's spirit was there—you could sense it everywhere in the garden and yard that she had so loved in life.

Red and I especially loved to get out and "play in the dirt" in the early spring, when the soil was warming up. We usually went barefoot and loved to feel the warm earth between our toes.

"Someone said that the best fertilizer is the farmer's footsteps, and I believe that's so," she once said.

She would water by hand most of the time, not wanting to get water on the leaves, as fungus is such a problem for plants in Florida. Also, watering each plant individually gave her the opportunity to weed them, to see if there were any pests on them, or to see if they needed fertilizing.

Although by nature very impatient, she mused, "One must not be in a hurry when gardening. You know, gardening and dogs both teach patience in their own way: dogs teach patience by example, gardening by force—no matter what you do, that corn is not going to grow any faster, nor the tomatoes turn red any quicker. You would think, surrounded as I am by both dogs and gardens, that I would be the most patient person alive. I guess I'm not a very good student." Admittedly, we all got impatient waiting for Red's sweet corn to ripen. To stand in Red's corn patch, eating crisp, raw, sugary, sweet corn was to know heaven.

One of Red's favorite pastimes in the grove was catching doodle bugs. One day when I was still very young, I saw her in her garden on hands and knees—not unusual, as she always had plenty of weeding to do. "Shrimpette," she beckoned, "come see this."

I went over and she showed me what she was doing. "See this little funnel shaped depression in the sand? Watch what happens when I dribble a few grains of sand into it." I watched intently as she did so, and a small bug pushed the sand up as it rose to the surface. "He thinks the sand is an ant caught in his trap, and is coming up to get him to eat for lunch."

Red scooped under the bug and held it in her hand. It was small, brown, and round, very ordinary looking. "This is the larva of the Ant Lion, and that's how he cleverly catches his prey." She called them doodle bugs, and catching them was always entertaining.

Red aspired to being a perfectionist in her yard, and tried to have something blooming there year-round. She even had plants that bloomed at night. She had a brilliant, magenta colored water lily in her pond, which only opened at night. She planted night blooming jasmine under the bedroom windows, the intoxicating aroma assuring sweet dreams for all. Our river road was also blessed with the wild, native cactus, the night -blooming *cereus.* These were square-shaped, long, linear cactus plants with short spines that climbed up into the cabbage palm and oak trees. Every June we looked forward to their blooming. For such a homely plant to produce such spectacular flowers was remarkable; Red said that was a good lesson—that sometimes the plainest packages contained the greatest beauty. When darkness fell, the flowers would open, so quickly you could see it happen with the naked eye, as if it were time-lapse photography. Each bloom lasted only one night. They were beautiful, large, white flowers with a soft fragrance, and by morning they would be closed, hanging limply from the cactus, their one night of glory over.

One winter when her great uncle was visiting, he took it upon himself to "clean out the palm trees"—to rid them of that ugly, thorny cactus growing on them, which he thought surely must be a parasite and harmful to the tree.

Red saw him and ran over, "Don't do that!" she exclaimed, "Those are the beautiful night-blooming cereus! In June they have incredibly gorgeous flowers and they don't hurt the trees at all."

She told me later it wasn't his fault—one had to understand that Yankees just didn't know any better. He had to be educated about our flora here down South. Red allowed "Being a Yankee" as an excuse for just about any kind of foolishness. Though she didn't much care for most of them, (most of her Mom's family were Northerners), she said we had to be tolerant of them, after all, they couldn't help where they were born, and not everyone could be as lucky as we were to be born in the South.

16—On Being Southern

One day I came home from school in tears. "There's a new boy in my class from New York," I sobbed, "he called me a little hick and a redneck."

"Don't worry," Red cooed, stroking my long braids, "he's just a Yankee, what does he know? They have many names for Southerners, like hayseed, redneck, hillbillly, covite, yokel, bumpkin, and cracker—I've heard them all. Northerners will never understand us, but that is their loss."

"Next time he calls you names, tell him with pride, 'Did you know that four of the first five presidents of the United States, seven of the first ten, and ten of the first sixteen, were Southerners? Did you know that George Washington, the father of our country, James Madison, the principal framer of the Constitution, and Thomas Jefferson, author of the Declaration of Independence, were Southern? Did you know that Peyton Randolph, President of the first Continental Congress, was from the South?' In reality, you could say that the foundation and the guiding philosophies of our great nation are largely those of our Southern forefathers, most of whom were English aristocrats."

"Furthermore, General Lee was, according to most military men, one of the greatest military geniuses of the Western world. So gifted a military strategist was he that military academies still study his tactics today, and so great a paragon of Southern gentility, he will never be forgotten by true Southerners." Red continued, "in fact, Robert E. Lee was the only West Pointer who ever graduated from there without one single demerit! Just you see what that Yankee smarty pants has to say to that! I'll bet he doesn't know his history so well after all. Shrimpette, as Southerners, we should be very proud of Lee and our other great Southern leaders. We do ourselves a great disservice to forget these men, or worse, not to stand up for them when their character is under assault by modern-day so-called historians."

"You see," she continued, "there are many reasons why Southerners are different. And there are many reasons to be proud to be a Southerner. First, Southerners traditionally were agrarians. This means they were farmers, and all that that entails—they loved the land and the soil and what it could bear. It has been said that the aristocratic life is based on ownership of land. The first settlers and farmers in the South were mostly landed English gentry, including George Washington, the Randolphs, and the Lees. Really, to a Southerner, ownership of land is the most important thing. Without it, you have nothing. As a matter of fact, fully one half of America's small farms, arguably our nation's backbone, are in the South, a region less than one fourth of our nation's land mass."

To Red, land was the only possession worth having. Being Southern to her was being rooted in the agrarian tradition. As she explained, the great dynasties of the south were built not on industrial wealth, but on cotton, timber, tobacco, and here in Florida, citrus and muck farming.

"You know, the largest farmland owners in the world, the Dudas, started right here in our backyard, making their first fortune growing celery," Red said.

Then she gave me a copy of *The Good Earth* by Pearl Buck to read. On the last page she had underlined Wang Lung, the dying patriarch's, speech to his sons: "It is the end of a family—when they begin to sell the land. Out of the land we came and into it we must go—and if you will hold your land you can live—no one can rob you of land—if you sell the land, it is the end."

"One reason that the land is so important to me and to other Southerners," continued Red, "is that it provides a family, a people, a society with roots." She giggled at her unintentional pun. "Just remember the words Margaret Mitchell gave to Gerald O'Hara in *Gone With the Wind*, 'The land, Scarlett, it's the land.'"

"When your roots are based in the land, they will always be there, there will be a continuum of your family and its heritage. Look at this house," she pointed out as we drove along the River Road, "the great grandfather of the present owner built that house and worked that orange grove behind it. In some strange way, it's very comforting to be able to say that—to know and associate with families that have a lengthy history in one place. We are also lucky to have that generational stability and continuity ourselves, Shrimpette. Our families, too, have been here a long time and there is a common and everlasting bond between us and all the other long-time natives because of it."

"The concept of honor has always been a recurrent theme in Southern life. That is not to say that we have a monopoly of honorable people down South," Red continued, "or that all Southerners are honorable— we all have our 'white trash' and hate-mongers to deal with—but old-time Southerners, from the elite to the working classes, all valued highly the virtue of honor and aspired to be honorable people. Why," Red said, "one of the South's preeminent university's motto is *ecce quam bonum*, which means, simply, to be that which is good."

"Red," I asked, "If Southerners were so honorable, what is so good or honorable about slavery? How was that justified?" Following Red's advice, at eleven years old, I was questioning everything.

Red responded, "First, Shrimpette, don't be so quick to judge our forbears. They were living in a different world, one where slavery worldwide was both commonplace and acceptable—and had always been, throughout the history of man—though that still does not make it right. Some modern historians argue that slavery in the South was slowly declining by the 1850's and that industrialization would eventually make it unfeasible. The war, in their opinion, hastened the end of slavery. The real tragedy was the tremendous loss of life, North and South, that marked this epic period of our history."

"Closely intertwined with the concept of honor," Red continued, "was that of the Southern gentleman and lady. Southerners were well known for their good breeding, manners, and hospitality—what we called gentility. In fact, General George Patton put it very well when he astutely noticed after enrolling at West Point, that, 'There are very few *born* gentlemen among the cadets and they are *all* Southerners.'"

"Really," Red explained, "what good manners boil down to is consideration for others, and putting others before yourself. A true Southern gentleman is a wonderful thing to encounter, and I feel sorry for all those girls who never met or will never meet one. And I really feel sorry for this new generation of feminists who cannot even tolerate a man opening the door for her! You see, the man is not doing that because he sees the woman as weak or incapable, but rather he has been taught to treat others with kindness and respect. And it's not only men in the South who open doors, by the way. A Southern lady will always open the door for an elderly, disabled, or incapacitated person, or children. Likewise they will also give up their seat for these same people. This is simply good manners, or 'good breeding' as we call it in the South." She sighed, "It's nice to know that chivalry still survives down here in the South."

"To me, the Southern gentleman and lady were a special blend of these concepts of gentility and honor, their like perhaps not to be seen again in our culture. Because these virtues were practically inborn in them, or at least engrained at an early age, they automatically carried the torch of something else sadly missing today—the idea *of noblesse oblige*" Red continued.

"Inherent in this ideal is that privilege entails responsibility; that is, the privileged classes have an obligation to be examples of high moral standards and of virtue and honor for everyone else to follow. Southern gentry used to take this responsibility very seriously, I believe. Once again, this idea probably came over with their aristocratic English ancestors."

"Why, even Shakespeare alluded to this in one of his sonnets, 'Lilies that fester smell far worse than weeds.' What he was saying," Red explained, "was that if a ghetto kid (a weed) gets into trouble, it is not too unexpected. Society does not look on him harshly. But when people with all the privileges do bad things, these 'lilies' of society really, really stink. Society expects more of them. It is very important in a free society that people born with advantages should set an example by being good, decent, honorable, and trustworthy. Likewise, those who are not born into privilege, but who do achieve fame and fortune later should also try hard to be role models for the underprivileged. Unfortunately, this concept of *noblesse oblige* has very much fallen by the wayside in our country now."

"Besides the agrarian tradition, Southern ladies and gentlemen, honor and chivalry, the South has always been famous for 'Southern hospitality,'" Red continued with her lesson in Southern culture.

"In the old South, it would be unthinkable not to invite someone in who dropped by to visit, regardless if they were strangers or friends. A Southerner's house was always open to friends, neighbors, relatives, and even to strangers."

Even during the Depression, Red's mom told us, hobos would stop at the door. No one turned them away, no one was afraid of them. The housewife would make them some food and they would be on their way. For their part, they did not steal or vandalize either. Some would also do a little work for their meal.

Almost always when friends would drop by for a visit, the Southern hostess would invite them to stay for tea, or other drinks (usually whisky, sometimes moonshine), and an assortment of snacks. And Sunday afternoons after church traditionally were the times most Southerners went calling on each other. Virtually everyone had an "open house" on Sunday, sitting on their verandas, catching up on the local gossip, the men sipping fine whisky and smoking cigars, the women sipping tea and eating dainties.

Naturally, Red had a theory to explain why Southerners were friendlier and their homes more inviting than their Northern counterparts. "Not only was their hospitality a result of inborn graciousness and good manners, but I believe that climate had much to do with it. I have observed this in other countries as well. For instance, northern Italians are much colder, more reserved, and not as friendly as their southern counterparts. Southern Italians are warm and welcoming, like Southern Americans. I think when a culture has a climate that allows them to be outdoors most of the time, people are just naturally friendlier. It just makes sense—you are outdoors, your neighbors also are outside, you talk across the fence, you wave to people passing by your house on the street, and you talk to them—strangers and friends alike. You are naturally more sociable when you are sitting on your balmy front porch than when you are shivering alone in your house with the doors and windows tightly shut."

"Well," she went on, "talk of Southern hospitality inevitably leads to talk of Southern cooking. Although Yankees like Aunt Loretta love to scoff at our 'cuisine'—or, as they would say, the lack of it—we know what we like.

Southern life has always been celebrated not only on the front porch sipping tea or whisky, but at the table with our own type of comestibles, mostly grown by our own hands. And, incidentally, much of our Southern style cooking is borrowed from African cooking learned from slaves."

"The first thing you learn about Southern eating is that dinner is lunch, and supper is never dinner, but the night meal. This is very confusing to anyone but Southerners! Lunch was called dinner because usually it was the main meal of the day. The farmers, often with their farm hands, or at least the field overseer, would leave the fields at noon and come into a magnificent spread of food. The women of the household had spent all morning cooking a glorious feast for the hungry workers. The dinner table, groaning under the weight, would typically be loaded down with two or three kinds of meat—all raised, butchered, and preserved on the farm—five or six vegetables grown in the nearby garden, homemade bread, real butter from the farmer's cows, and a couple of Mama's best pies, made with whatever kind of fruit that was in season, to top it all off. In the summer, there was often home-made ice cream, hand cranked in a churn, or ice-cold watermelon or other homegrown fruits and melons. Southerners have always been pretty much self-sufficient when it comes to growing or hunting for their food."

"Some Southern favorites were collard greens, field peas cooked all day with ham hock, biscuits, corn bread, spoon bread, corn pone, candied yams, grits (Red's dad called grits Georgia ice cream, usually eaten at breakfast), and of course fried chicken, fried okra, and fried catfish. Often wild game such as duck, dove, quail, venison, rabbit, or squirrel were served as well. And most things were best when smothered with 'pot likker,' or thick meat gravies, such as the delicious red eye gravy made from the drippings of fresh baked ham."

"Some of the regional specialties in these parts of Florida have been cooter (freshwater turtle), frog legs, avocado and tomato sandwiches, key lime pie, fritters of all kinds, hush puppies, wild fox grape or scuppernong jelly, mulberry preserves, calamondin preserves, and guava jelly. Original pioneers even ate sea turtles and manatees."

"Why, when I was little," Red mused, "I remember the fire station siren went off every day exactly at noon, and that signaled it was time to come in for my guava jelly and butter sandwich, my preferred lunch."

"To this day, guava jelly is my favorite. Perhaps I love it so much because it is so difficult to make it well. Making good guava jelly is a two day proposition and I just don't have the patience for it. Fortunately, I have good friends who make it, and I am happy to supply them with the guavas to do it."

Red's dad, too, loved "gobber" jelly, as he called it. He was also very partial to goober peas (peanuts) and peanut butter, watermelon, and mangoes. When he discovered that neither Red nor Duncan cared for those things, he claimed they must not be his children after all. Meanwhile, Red's mom could not understand how Red or Duncan could be *her* children and not like crabs, fish, or avocadoes. "We have some strange children, Pa. I think the nurses must have switched them at birth with someone else's kids," she would sigh and shake her head, meanwhile eating her *dinner* of fresh stone crabs and avocado.

17—The Kids' Club

Red's attic was a wondrous place: it was always very warm and full of old steamer trunks, hat boxes, antiques, and many other curious things from her grandparents' day. Red figured it would make a perfect clubhouse for the neighborhood kids. In one end of the attic, everything was cleared out except what was needed for the clubhouse—trunks for a desk, tables and stools. Red made lists and drew on an antique chalkboard that had neat stuff to learn about on a large scroll that could be wound and unwound.

Red dubbed this space "The Rebels' Club," and any kid was eligible to join. Red was, of course, the unquestioned leader and president.

Under her leadership, many things were accomplished, for Red was a natural born organizer: Money was made in various ways, regular meetings were held, and the most notable accomplishment, a weekly newspaper was published. It was called the *Chit Chat* and had a circulation of about twenty, and several papers even went out of state. Red had a successful sales formula for increasing circulation—write "news" (aka gossip) about all the neighbors, and they would have to buy the paper to see what might have been written about themselves! Her plan worked like a charm and all the neighborhood became subscribers.

Each kid was responsible for a "section" of the paper. Red did the news and editing; someone else had a page of jokes, and another kid had an almanac page with the weather, pithy sayings, and recipes now and then. The Patrick Air Force weather service would always be called to get the latest weather update. The last page was one of advertisements, which were also sold to bring in income.

It started out that each copy was laboriously written out by hand each week, severely limiting the number of copies that could be produced. Then, Red's grandfather sent her a "hectograph" so that many copies could be printed more expeditiously. This hectograph was actually nothing more than a tray of gelatin.

Each kid would write his section by hand with a special colored pencil. Then the page was put face down onto the gelatin for fifteen or twenty minutes. The gelatin would absorb the printing, and then blank pages would be put on, one after another, lifting the print off the gelatin onto the paper. Then all the pages would be assembled, stapled together, and they were ready for delivery, which was done on bikes.

Some of the newsworthy snippets were:

"Patty R's horse escaped last night and ended up in Mrs. Ruffner's front yard, eating her daisies and pooping on her geraniums."

"The Smiths have a new color TV set. It does not show color all the time, just when the program is in color."

"Mike W. has the mumps."

"Red's dog, Shadow, stole Mr. Miller's pants off the clothes line and Red had to go around the neighborhood to find the owner."

On the joke-almanac-recipe page, one could find "If at first you don't fricasee, fry, fry a hen!" Or "Recipe for Ciber Jelly: boil ciber to the consistency of syrup, and let it cool, and you have a nice jelly." The little boy responsible for that section obviously had trouble remembering his d's and b's.

114

Every so often the paper would have an obituary column, mostly with notices of various people's pets' deaths, even including the chickens.

"Red's old hen disappeared during the day, and her daughter had four chicks which a skunk got last night."

Everyone, it seems, knew the genealogy of the chickens.

One obituary read, "Red's dog, only nine months old, was killed by a speeding motorcycle, who didn't even slow down. Red's new puppy is being sent by train from Nebraska and there will be a contest to name her. The winner will be awarded 10 cents or a free issue of the *Chit Chat*. Things to consider: a) female dog b) golden color c) hunting dog d) good Southern name."

Our neighbor, Mrs. McDonald won the contest with the high-falootin' name of "Red's Goldeness Madchen," which means "Red's Golden Girl" in German. Of course, this was to be her AKC registered name. Her everyday name was just Dixie.

Mrs. McDonald was an appropriate person to win the contest, as she was a dog lover herself, and a big supporter of the club and paper. Not wanting to miss the news, one supposes, she even kept her *Chit Chat* subscription year-round and Red sent her the summer issues to her home up north.

There is a theory that dogs and their owners come to look like each other after a while, and it was certainly true in Mrs. McDonald's case. She was a winter resident from New Jersey, rather corpulent, and she always wore loose jersey dresses, hose rolled down to the knee, and clunky black shoes with chunky heels, popular with elderly women in those days. Like many ladies of that age, she always had a hankie stuffed somewhere deep down in her ample bosom which could be miraculously produced when needed. Like herself, her dog never missed a meal—her owner made sure of it. Her "Duchess" was a very rotund black cocker spaniel with droopy eyelids and saggy jowls, very much like her owner. If she even so much as glanced at her food dish, her mistress, perhaps sympathizing with her hunger, would fill it with succulent treats. Dog and mistress waddled around the house together and occasionally padded out to the mailbox.

Mrs. McDonald had no children and she loved Red. Red liked her too, and not just because she sent her money for her birthday and Christmas. She did many nice things for Red, including teaching her how to knit. A dear lady, with a heart as big as her figure, Mrs. McDonald kept Red and her family supplied with those warm, wool, knitted slippers that they all loved, and she was always knitting sweaters for her husband. Under her expert tutelage, Red eventually knitted two mohair sweaters herself. One

turned out all right, but too heavy for Florida's balmy climes. The second one was not as heavy, but ended up with two very long sleeves, one being about six inches longer than the other. Since Red's mom had long limbs, she was given the sweater, and she would just roll up the longer sleeve when she wore it, looking rather like she had just come from the thrift store.

But back in the clubhouse, Red, always the inventor, had better success. She came up with an ingenious way to keep the members supplied with snacks while attending meetings or working on the paper. The clubhouse was two stories directly above the back kitchen door, thus making it too remote for numerous "cookie runs." Red devised a little tray, hung by a rope, which she would lower out the clubhouse window down to the kitchen door, two stories below. The tray had a bell attached to the bottom of it and Red would jiggle the rope, jingling the bell. Her mother would open the back door and put cookies in the tray, which would then be hoisted up for all to enjoy. Her mother was always a good sport.

Sometimes her mom would be sewing in the room just below the attic club house. It was all she could do not to laugh out loud as the young club members very seriously "Pledged allegiance to the flag of the Rebel's Club of River Road, with liberty and justice for all Rebels."

As few of us had TVs, we had active imaginations, and that, plus Red's conservative fiscal policy, evinced even then at her young age, ensured that the club always had money in its piggy bank. Actually, her family all accused her of being the family miser, so good was she at saving her money. Besides the newspaper, one of the ways the club "raised" money was to collect empty Coke and Pepsi bottles along the roads. US 1 was usually a good source for "empties." The tall guinea grass alongside the road was usually replete with soda bottles. They were turned in for a two cent refund each. The members also made potholders on those little metal looms and sold them for a quarter apiece.

Red's brother, being older, was not interested in the club or the paper, but he did make fun of them when he could, just to get Red riled up.

"You know, Red, the big paper in Atlanta has the motto "Covers Dixie like the Dew." Your paper could have the motto "Covers River Road like the dog doo!" — he said one day, smirking.

Duncan laughed uproariously at his own joke.

Red retaliated, lips pursed determinedly, chin stuck out defiantly, "You just wait, Duncan. I'm going to be famous one day! You'll see!" And so it came to be, and much sooner than even Red imagined.

It so happened that a very well-known columnist for the Miami Herald mentioned a hectograph in his column one day. Reading about it prompted Red to send him a copy of the *Chit Chat* and tell him about how it was produced — with a hectograph. Very shortly, he wrote a whole column about Red, the hectograph and the *Chit Chat*. So, for a brief moment, Red *was* famous.

As the kids got older and pursued other diversions, interest waned in the club and the paper. Perhaps the old copies of the paper might be collectors' items today if there were any copies still extant. Certainly anyone who ever read them will never forget the *Chit Chat*.

18—A Dog's Life

Red was a very spiritual person, but her "religion," was a curious admixture of Eastern mysticism, Christianity, and Hellenic philosophy, with a healthy dose of animism thrown in. She avowed her confirmed faith in a supreme being, and said we all needed to answer to a higher authority — and, she joked, that didn't mean the IRS.

"Shrimpette," she said, still instructing me even though I was now a college student, "I believe all of the world's many religions have something good to say to us, they all have some divine, instructive, and timeless truths that can be gleaned from them."

She also thought that most of the world's great civilizations had been built on the backs of one religion or another — Islam, Confucianism, and Catholicism, to name a few.

"Of course," she carefully noted, "we must not forget that our great civilization here in America was built solidly on Judeo-Christian ethics and morals, which explains a lot of what we are all about, and why things are the way they are in this country — why we enjoy such great freedom and why we are the greatest nation on earth."

Red did not like organized religious groups and did not go to church, preferring, like Emily Dickinson, to

> ...keep the Sabbath...staying at home
> With a bobolink for a Chorister
> And an Orchard, for a Dome....

"To put yourself in a higher authority's hands, and not to have to worry anymore about the course of your life was 'the truth that set you free,'" Red maintained.

She averred that once you understood that, then the only choice that was truly yours was that of being good or evil, and then the only onus on you was to be good. Of course, choosing whether to be good or evil can be a great burden, and God has given us free will to make that incredibly important choice for ourselves. The Hindus believe in a law of moral nature, which is called *karma*. The Christians put it so well, "As ye sow, so shall ye reap."

Red believed intuitively and deeply that the purpose of human life was the search for truth — and thereby the discovery of and the union with God.

"Of course," she expained, "this is nothing new — this tenet is at the core of almost every great religion in the world. Man is given a mind to acquire knowledge — to use his wisdom to contemplate truth. Plato identifies *the good* with knowledge, and as such, virtue is not an end in itself, but the indispensable means to knowing God. Inherent in the Hindu *Bhagavad Gita* is the truism that right action is the way to knowledge, and therefore to heaven, as it purifies the mind and enables it to intuit God — to 'know' the ineffable."

Red believed that dogs were at the higher end of the spiritual scale of evolution — that, with just one more 'spin of the wheel,' dogs would escape the birth and rebirth cycle called *sansara* and be reunited with God. She thought so highly of dogs that she had to believe they were just one step below God.

Grinning, she said, "That's why dog is god spelled backwards."

She was fond of telling the story of Yudhisthira, one time ruler of India: "When Yudhisthira journeyed far to reach heaven, accompanied by his faithful dog, he was told by Indra, Lord of the Gods, that the dog was not allowed inside. Yudhisthira answered that if that was so, he had no wish to enter, as he could not desert a trusting creature who only wished for his protection. Finally, both were allowed in, and the dog was revealed as Dharma (Sanskrit for 'right action') himself."

This parable of Hindu philosophy meant a lot to Red, and I heard her say many times, "It will not be heaven to me unless my loyal dogs are there with me — it could have every other luxury in the universe, but if they weren't there, it would be my hell."

There was no doubt in her mind that dogs and other animals had souls, and she would quote Byron (one of her favorite poets, because he so obviously loved dogs):

> ...But the poor dog, in life the firmest friend
> First to welcome, foremost to defend
> Unhonored falls, unnoticed all his worth
> Denied in heaven the soul he held on earth,

> While man, vain insect, hopes to be forgiven
> And claims himself a sole, exclusive heaven....

As long as I had known them, Red's family always had Labrador Retrievers. The beautiful, smart Shadow was the dog of her childhood. Duncan named him after "The Shadow," and Red and Duncan about drove their mom nuts constantly saying, "Who knows these things?—the Shadow knows." It turned out to be a very appropriate name, as he *was* the kids' shadow, especially Red's. He followed her everywhere, determined to protect her. Shadow was a male yellow Lab with every possible good trait you could ask for in a dog, and none of the bad. For he had, as Red would quote, again from Byron:

> ...Beauty without vanity,
> Strength without insolence,
> Courage without ferocity,
> And all the virtues of man
> *Without* his vices...

Shadow was our pal, and Red's best friend and protector. He was also the neighborhood rascal. Back in the days before heavy traffic and leash laws, Shadow had free range of our town and he was the number one male dog. Often he would disappear for days at a time, returning all battered and thin. A female dog had been in heat—perhaps miles away—and he had been there doing his best to pass on his genes. He was a good fighter and very brave, and he would've defended Red to the death, of that there was no doubt. Red was his favorite: he idolized her, and she adored him. He always waited with her in the morning to get on the school bus and sometimes he would sneak on and ride to school with her, a couple of miles away. There, he would delight the kids by drinking out of the water fountain, then he would wander back home, greeting her as she stepped off the bus in the afternoon.

That dog was a natural born retriever and very intelligent— he could retrieve ducks that he hadn't seen shot down, and often he would get two birds on one retrieve—and all this with no formal training. Red's dad just took him along from the time he was old enough not to get in the way, and he took to it like a mullet takes to mud. Although in his later years he really disliked the cold water on his old, arthritic bones, he reluctantly would jump in and never failed to get his duck—it was a matter of pride to him.

He lived twelve years—throughout Red's childhood, and was actually a very important influence in her life. Because of having Shadow at an early age, she learned to respect animals for their nobility, stoicism, loyalty, and beauty, and thought man should strive to emulate them. For this reason she also believed that every kid ought to have a dog.

She was fond of quoting the *Bhagavad-Gita*, "Who sees his Lord within every creature, deathlessly dwelling amidst the mortal: That man sees truly."

Shadow lived to be a ripe old age and went down very fast at the end. His death affected her entire family, but her the most. They all cried over his demise, and the whole neighborhood mourned his passing. Mr. Dewey gave Red a white hibiscus from his nursery on Merritt Island, which she planted on Shadow's grave. As with all her animals, Red had a funeral, at which she recited Byron's epitaph for his Newfoundland dog,

> ...Ye, who perchance behold this simple urn, pass on.
> It honors none you wish to mourn.
> To mark a friend's remains these stones arise
> I never knew but one, and here he lies...

Red had been to Byron's home at Newstead Abbey in England, and had visited the grave of his beloved dog, Boatswain, with the inscribed poem on it. She could recite the long poem from memory.

Red said, in retrospect, she was just glad that Shadow was able to live his whole life free, with no fences or leash laws or traffic on the roads. He was able to follow Red on her bike, to visit the neighbors, to chase the rabbits and squirrels, or to take a swim in the river. Things would not always be that way for her dogs, or for us either.

After Shadow, they had a succession of several Labs, both yellow and black, all of them equally as dear to Red as he had been. One of them she named Argus. I asked Red where the name Argus came from.

"Argus was the dog of Ulysses," Red explained, "and was the only member of the family to recognize him when he returned after twelve years of wandering. Argus was old and ill, but held on until his master returned, wagged his tail on recognition of the disguised Ulysses, then died a happy dog. No one else in the household had recognized Ulysses."

Red loved to tell that tale, and after I heard it the first time, she gave me copies of *The Iliad* and *The Odyssey* to read, all dog-eared and well-underlined.

The dog of Red's young adult life was a black female dog she called Polly-wog. She was called that because as a puppy she was fat, black, and soft, just like a big fat pollywog. Polly was only half Lab, the rest a mixture of Shepherd, Husky, and wolf. By now, Red was convinced that most breeds of purebred dogs had been ruined by excessive in-breeding and over-breeding by people who knew nothing about dogs or genetics. She now swore only by mixed breeds, feeling they possessed "hybrid vigor." And if Polly was any example, I'd have to agree with her. She was a lovely, strong, healthy, intelligent dog with great heart. Red got her at five weeks of age and they were constant companions all Polly's life — sixteen years. Polly went with Red everywhere, even to work, and she joked that she always had to buy a car with Polly in mind: the dog had to have a back seat with a window that would go down all the way, for she loved to hang her head out the window, ears flapping back, nose in the wind. Polly loved riding in the car with Red almost better than anything, and Red referred to her car as "Polly's dog house on wheels." When riding around, if it was her meal time, or if she had to go to the bathroom, she would rest her muzzle on Red's shoulder and sigh. Red said that animals were smarter than humans because they could be taught our language, but we never could understand theirs. Red, however, did learn Polly's way of communicating after many years together. In her wonderfully unobtrusive, unpresumptuous, doggy way, Polly pretty much ruled Red's life for many years and brought her much joy. Of course, Red had a theory about their mutual happiness.

"You know, Shrimpette," she said, "I ought to write a book on happiness — that is, I believe if everyone would strive to give their dogs a happy life, they would also be happy. Think about it — if you only did things that made your dog happy, what a great life you would have — hiking in the woods, swimming in the river, throwing balls and sticks in the fresh air and sunshine. Think how much healthier we'd be, too. So I think I have come up with the key to happiness — do things to please and amuse your dog, and you will be amused also."

"I also have a theory about how people could eat healthier," she continued. "Think of all the times people have told you, 'Don't feed that to your dog — it's not good for him!' Usually they are referring to a potato chip or a piece of candy. Then they proceed to eat it themselves. Does it make sense that it would not be good for your dog, but good for you? I think, of course, that dogs can eat almost anything we eat safely, but, in fact, certain foods are not too healthy for dogs or for us. Yet, we will eat the junk foods while admitting they aren't healthy for our dog! My theory is that if you have

123

something you wouldn't feed your dog, you probably would be better off not eating it either. So, people could be much healthier if they would only feed themselves what would be okay to feed their dog."

"I have another theory about dogs and people," she continued. "If every kid had to learn to drive a car while carrying a dog in the back seat, people would be better drivers and we would have fewer accidents. You see, when you have a dog in the car, you cannot start and stop suddenly, you cannot turn corners too sharply or too fast. You are forced to pay attention, because any sudden movement of the car will have your dog tumbling all over the place and hurting himself. With a dog in the car, you are forced to drive slowly and carefully and more attentively."

"In short, it seems that if humans would live according to a dog's needs, we would all be happier, healthier, and safer. I think that Franz Kafka was right when he said 'All knowledge, the totality of all questions, and all answers, is contained in the dog.'"

Polly was quite a huntress in her younger days. She had a beautiful way of running, her sleek, muscular body effortlessly galloping and jumping over puddles, rocks, and tree limbs. She was very curious, too, always putting her nose in holes and hollow logs and sniffing bushes. She easily ran down rabbits and squirrels. She routinely caught 'possums and was quite fearless even against raccoons and snakes, never backing down.

When she was young, and stayed outside at night, Polly became a great escape artist. Red and her dad kept increasing the height of the backyard fence, and Polly kept finding a way over or under. She was a very athletic jumper, and could clear a five foot fence easily. She also could climb trees, especially liking to climb the old mulberry in Red's back yard. She was especially apt to escape on full-moon nights, and she would hunt all night in the groves and woods behind Red's house. In the morning she would show up very tired and would sleep half the day.

Once when we were walking in the grove, Polly stopped, looked at the ground, head cocked to the side, standing still like a statue. "Watch what happens next," Red whispered. She had seen this many times. Polly suddenly started to dig, and within seconds, lifted a little grey mole out of the dirt. How she knew it was there was a mystery — did she smell it, hear it, feel it beneath her feet? Red jokingly said she should rent Polly out as a mole catcher, as many people didn't like them in their yards. Red always said that if Polly got lost in the woods she would be able to survive, she was such a good hunter.

Red was a diligent observer of animal behavior and she learned a lot from Polly. One cold day while she, Polly, and I were lying in the grass soaking up some warm Florida sunshine, Red shared some of her observations with me.

"Did you ever notice how Polly always sleeps with her back against me and her rear end by my face? And when she lies beside my bed at night, it is always with her back end by my bed, her head pointing toward the door. You see, in nature, two dogs can lie together back to back and head to tail and protect themselves quite well. It is all so beautifully instinctual—they each protect each other's backs, and with their heads at each end, they have a very wide range of vision to see any attackers that may approach."

"And have you noticed that she always has to be in the lead when we are walking or hiking. It has always been that way, since she reached adulthood. She is very much the *alpha* female, the leader of the pack."

Even in her old age, when she could only meander slowly about the place, she would still cut in front of Red when they were walking, forcing Red to walk very slowly behind her.

Red talked to the old dog as if she were human, "Polly, you have always been in front, leading me. When you were young you would have to wait for me to catch up to you. One thing you have tried to teach me by example is patience. You are always waiting for me—waiting for me to come home, waiting patiently in the car, waiting to be fed, waiting for me to get up in the

morning, always patiently waiting. You remind me of Milton's poem, 'They also serve, who only stand and wait.' I reckon you will go ahead before me to the great beyond also—be patient and wait for me there. I will try to behave myself and be good, so that I can join you someday."

When Polly had become quite old, she became arthritic and rather frail— she was paying for her youthful athleticism with her worn out legs. Red would cater to her every need, just as if she were an infant. When Polly could no longer make it up the stairs at night to sleep beside Red's bed, Red moved downstairs and slept on the floor with Polly. When Red was doting on her, her mom would say, "Red, you're never going to get a man when he sees you kissing on that dog—the man wants to be the center of your attention, and not be second to a dog."

Red just laughed and said, "Well, if I could find a man even half as loyal, devoted, and loving as Polly, then he would understand. If a man was jeal-ous of Polly, I would just tell him what Shakespeare said about old age and approaching death, 'This thou perceivest, which makes thy love more strong/ To love that *well* which thou must leave ere long.' Not only that, but I don't think I could possibly be interested in any man that didn't love dogs—in fact, I am very leery of anyone who claims not to like dogs—it shows a serious character flaw, if you ask me!"

"Besides," added Red, "now that Polly's old and at times difficult to care for, am I supposed to do away with her, just because she's become inconve-nient? I wouldn't do that to you Mom! When I took her as a pup, I signed on for life, *her life*, not just till it becomes inconvenient to care for her. It's true, we live in a throwaway society now, but just because she's old and broken down, I will not replace her with a newer model!"

Her mom just shook her head and said, "I hope when I die that I will be reincarnated as one of Red's dogs—that would be the best life imagin-able!"

As Polly declined with advancing age, Red watched helplessly as her best friend slipped off into the netherland of Shakespeare's void: "sans eyes, sans teeth, sans taste, sans everything." The old dog and her master walked every evening and their evening constitutionals became slower and shorter until they walked no more. Polly was too feeble.

In Polly's descent into that silent, darkening world of cataracts and deaf-ness, that twilight of life, Red glimpsed her own mortality for the first time, and she prayed that in her last days she would have someone as devoted to her as she was to Polly, someone to hold her hand as she tran-spired from this world to another level of being. At sixteen years of age,

Polly died, leaving a huge void in Red's life, but she was wise enough to know that death was an unavoidable part of life.

Red had Polly's remains cremated and had strict instructions written into her will that when she passed on her ashes were to be mixed with Polly's. These remains were to be scattered upon the Indian River where they had roamed and played together for so many happy years. Red and Polly, inseparable in life, would be together always.

19—Travels with Red

Some years after I had moved from our River Road, I was cleaning out an old desk and came across a box of old post cards and letters sent to me by Red from her travels around the world. Among them was a long letter she had written from Morocco.

"Good grief," Red wrote me, "what were we thinking? We could have been sold in the *casbah* for slaves and no one would have known it!"

This smacked of another one of Red's outrageous adventures and I re-read the letter with both delight and a touch of sadness.

She had woken up in the berth of a sleeper train, at first not quite sure where she was. Her eyes squinted in the bright sun of Andalusia that was streaming in through the train window, and she remembered she was headed for North Africa.

She and her college roommates had been traveling to Madrid from Paris when they met two young men from Morocco. These nice young men—also students—had convinced Red and her friends to come home with them to Rabat, the capital of Morocco. "Let us show you the good things in Morocco—ours is not a dangerous country."

Always an adventurer, with little hesitation, Red voted to go. After all, one of the girls could speak French, so it would be all right. Now the train had pulled into Algeciras, at the bottom of Spain, to unload its passengers, most of whom were getting on the ferry to cross the Straits of Gibraltar to Tangiers. It was a rough crossing, but Red enjoyed being on the sea again. At Tangiers they boarded another train bound for the capital city of Rabat, home of their host, Chaker. His cousin had gone home to Fez, where the girls would go to visit him subsequently.

Arriving at Rabat very late at night, Chaker put the girls up at a dilapidated, rather seedy hotel. He didn't know what else to do. For it turned out that his was a Berber family from way out in the Atlas mountains. They, like many others, had moved into the city to find work and to supposedly better their lives. The father was a very old man who sewed *djellabas*, the robes that almost everyone wore over their clothes. Being so aged, and from the mountains, he was very conservative—that is, having three blue-jean clad, "wild" American girls in his house would be pushing him to the limits. The girls were blissfully unaware of any problems they might have caused in the household.

They were unaware because the father put aside any misgivings he might have had about these foreign "hussies," and true to his generous, hospitable, Berber nature, opened his house to them: they were his guests and that was that. Chaker's mother scolded him for leaving the girls in the ratty hotel and insisted that they stay with the family.

Now that sounds all well and good, but the family—mother, father, Chaker, his sister, and three or four nieces and nephews—was exceedingly poor. They all lived in a two room apartment, with a toilet (a hole in the floor) outside by the stairs, which served all the residents of that floor. They were so poor that there was only one light on the ceiling, with a very dim bulb, to light their small, bare two rooms. This was accomplished by cutting a square hole in the wall beside the light bulb so the light would shine into both rooms. Furniture consisted of cushions on the floor to sit or sleep upon.

In spite of their poverty, they saw to it that their guests lacked for nothing that they might want—they fed them those huge, sweet doughnuts called *beignets* in the morning and delicious *couscous* for dinner. Red had never tasted anything like it. Their hospitality overwhelmed the girls.

After a brief visit to Fez, with its colorful, huge *medina,* and numerous trips around Rabat to beautiful gardens, fascinating Arab cemeteries, King Hassan IIs palace, and other scenic spots, Chaker's sister took them to the communal baths. There was one for men and a separate one for women. They had not bathed in over a week. What an experience that was, Red wrote. For about fifty cents, a lady washed their hair and scrubbed them up and down, rinsing them by pouring buckets of warm water over them. She scrubbed so hard and with such an abrasive cloth, the girls were crying out, and all the other women in the baths were laughing at them—these Arab women had never seen "Western" women. They came out all washed and squeaky clean, and glad of it, for they had really needed a bath.

Rabat, like most Arab cities, also had a large *medina,* called a *casbah* by some, or in Turkey, a *bazaar.* Red loved to shop in these bazaars around the world and was in her element haggling over prices. The girls bought all kinds of wonderful things, including *djellabas,* pointed slippers, bloomers, and under-gowns—typical clothing of native women. Because they were next going to visit Chaker's family in the mountains, wearing "Western" clothes was *verboten*. The girls had to dress as natives, including covering their hair with scarves or special hoods that matched their *djellabas*. They were allowed to wear hiking boots or tennis shoes, as they would be doing a lot of walking over rough terrain in the mountains, although the Berbers only wore pointy little leather slip-on shoes no matter where they went.

Once a year, when Chaker came home from school in Paris, he would take as many of his family as he could pay for to the family headquarters deep in the Atlas mountains. This year he could only afford to take two sisters, so Red paid to take two of his young nieces, Kadijah and Fatima, along. By this time, one of the American girls had returned to Europe—the one who spoke French. So Chaker started to teach the other two Berber. Between Red's broken French, Berber, and hand language, they managed to get along, sometimes with hilarious results.

After a long bus ride to Marrakesh, the group boarded another bus to Imil Tanout, a small town in the Atlas mountains. Red noted that these mountains were very ancient, and one could tell that because they were rounded and blunt in shape, not sharp and jagged like our Rockies, which are much younger mountains. Upon arriving, they hiked a couple miles to the family compound. A large family of cousins awaited them there. Theirs was a typical Berber dwelling—a mud and stone, flat-roofed structure, built in a square pattern. One side of the square was living quarters for one family, one side for another family, a third side was a stable. The fourth side was a wall, and inside the square, which was probably fifty feet on each side, was the courtyard. Here the laundry was hung, the donkey and chickens roamed, and the women washed clothes and cooked. An oven was formed out of clay on the ground with a round hole on the side about a foot in diameter. Into it was put wood to burn, and in it the women baked the best bread Red had ever eaten. The *kobh*, or bread, was round and flat—about an inch thick. Every day they would bake it fresh. Bread was the most important part of the meal: Lacking eating utensils, a piece of bread was used to scoop up the *couscous*.

Outside the compound, on the back of one wall was built a smaller wall. Behind this wall was the outdoor potty, where a person simply squatted on the ground. On the other side of the compound was a hand dug well with a bucket on a rope. The girls would haul up water and wash their hair. They had no baths while they were in the mountains. Unfortunately, Red believed, the well was too close to the loo. Both girls got very ill with dys-

entery while there. They were so weak from "running at both ends," that they were afraid they wouldn't get back to school on time. Red was pretty sure that contamination of the well-water from the toilet area was probably the cause of their dysentery.

The Atlas mountains were beautiful, and unlike anything Red had ever seen. They were very arid and barren, their rounded tops and sides covered with rock and rubble and prickly pear cactus. The air was hot in the daytime and cool at night. There were no trees to speak of, but where there was a creek or a water source, people grew beautiful gardens. Among other things, they grew corn and the best melons Red had ever eaten. On the outside they were yellow with longitudinal, indented lines. Inside they were similar to our cantaloupe and honeydew melons, only even more sweet and succulent.

Often people took tea in their vegetable gardens. Mint tea was the national beverage. It was made simply by boiling water, then adding mint leaves and sugar. And Moroccans drank it often—for every meal and whenever anyone came to visit. There was always tea for guests, and later Red would see just how important to their culture tea was.

One day, Chaker and his cousin Brahim decided they would take the girls to a Berber wedding of a friend many miles away. They left in late afternoon, taking two donkeys for Red and her friend to ride. The men walked, leading the animals, and Red felt like Mary on the flight to Egypt. Soon it turned dark and upon looking upward, Red saw so many stars, she couldn't believe they were on the same planet as at home. There was virtually no pollution out there and no lights, so that it seemed every star in the galaxy was visible. The route was very dark, and Red could only see shadows of plants along the way—they turned out to be prickly pear cactus, which the natives liked to eat. Red was not impressed with the fruit—they were mildly sweet, but too full of seeds. It was a good thing the girls could not see their surroundings that night, for the path snaked between steep precipices on one side, and cactus covered mountainsides on the other.

Upon arrival, it was already quite late, but the festivities were just beginning. This was the second night of a three night celebration. This was the night of gift giving. The festivities were held in the courtyard, and onlookers, including Red's group, could watch the goings-on from the surrounding flat roofs —the best vantage point. First, there was a lot of the peculiar, high-pitched singing and wailing by the women, along with clapping and much jingling of their silver jewelry. The women were dressed in typical multi-layered dresses, quite colorful, with lots of dangly silver necklaces and bracelets.

After much ululating and clapping, the gift giving began. To Red's surprise, most people gave one of two things—money or sugar. Chaker explained to them that sugar was a very valuable commodity because of the ubiquitous tea drinking; if a guest had no sugar to give, they would purchase some of the sugar that had already been given as gifts, then give it back. This way, they gave the bride and groom sugar *and* money. The sugar came in huge chunks, in perfect conical form, maybe a foot high, and wrapped in blue paper. The giving of sugar went on most of the rest of the night, and in the wee hours the girls fell asleep on the rooftop.

When the sun came up, bright and hot over the eastern horizon, it was time to go home. That evening, the party would continue, but the girls had to leave. When they had gotten out of range of the house, Red asked Chaker, *"Ou est le bain?"*—where is the bath(room)? He shook his head and said, *"No, non ici— a la maison. "* Red argued with him, for by this time, the girls' bladders were as full as they could be. She protested, *"Por quoi non ici?"*— why not here?— for there was no one in sight, and there were lots of prickly pears and other scrubby bushes to hide them. She was getting desperate. Finally, Chaker started laughing, *"Ah, la toilette!"* Red had asked for a bath, not a bathroom. They stopped *tout suite,* and the girls relieved themselves behind a cactus, being careful not to get a prickly pear in their behind.

The next day, Chaker and Brahim took the girls to their local "village," really just a few houses clustered together on a hillside. One of these houses was that of the local silversmith. The girls went in, and after the obligatory tea, and after much haggling over the price, bought some jewelry—hand-made silver rings and bracelets.

They then walked home, up and down rocky hillsides with herds of goats and little children watching over them. Chaker told the girls that an airport was slated to be built in the nearest large village—to bring in tourists, more people, and development. He was all for it—that meant prosperity.

Red argued with him, "Take it from me, I come from a place with lots of people and development—you don't want that here. Your beautiful mountains will not stay that way. Your serene, quiet existence will be forever altered by the noise of the planes, by pollution, and strangers."

She shook her head in despair at the thought. Her protests didn't seem to change his mind. Her only hope was that perhaps this place was so remote that it wouldn't happen soon.

One morning, the girls awoke to a very solemn procession leaving from a neighboring house and walking slowly past theirs. Everyone was dressed in black, and four men were carrying a stretcher draped with a large cloth. Chaker explained that a woman in that house had been stung by a scorpion, which killed her. They were going to bury her. The girls were on the look-out thereafter for the deadly venomous insect. Apparently scorpions were fairly common in the dry mountains, and as everyone slept on the floor, they were definitely something to be feared.

On their last hike in the mountains, much to her shock and dismay, Chaker asked Red's roommate to marry him! Of course she had no intentions of doing that, and they learned later that women like her were in great demand, and highly prized in that part of the world—she had beautiful blue eyes, which was something so rare that it was the measure of beauty there.

After spending more than three weeks in Morocco, the girls had to be getting back to Europe and school. But first they had to leave the mountains. They got on the bus for the long ride back to Rabat with tears in their eyes. Their Berber hosts had been so kind, they hoped they would see them again some day.

As I solemnly put the letter back in the box, I thought about how Red loved to travel above all else.

Red could never understand people who had no wanderlust, no curiosity about the wide world, no desire to know other lands, peoples and cultures. But she was, at the same time, glad that not everyone liked to travel, or else there would be even more tourists than there already were.

"Shrimpette," she often recited to me,

> "...When all the world is young, lad,
> And all the trees are green;
> And every goose a swan, lad,
> And every lass a queen;
> Then hey for boot and horse, lad,
> And 'round the world away;
> Young blood must have its course, lad,
> And every dog his day.
>
> ...When all the world is old, lad,
> And all the trees are brown;
> And all the sport is stale, lad,

135

And all the wheels run down;
Creep home and take your place, there, The spent
and maimed among:
God grant you find one face, there,
You loved when all was young."

"Shrimpette," she asserted, "like Charles Kingsley said, see the world while you are young, especially the more remote and underdeveloped areas. Travel is difficult, but rewarding in these places, but not too easy for old people. You can see Europe and the United States when you are old — travel is easy there. Besides, many of these places are beginning to change rapidly, and it is best to see them while they are still untouched by Western ways. Get out and see the wide world, there will be plenty of time later to potter in your garden."

She also advised me, "Take poetry with you wherever you go. Travel and poetry greatly enrich one's life, and like dogs, poetry helps to keep away the loneliness. I hate to think of my life without the delight of poetry — like Keats said, 'A thing of beauty is a joy forever.' Like travel and dogs, poetry has brought much joy to my life."

Of course, Red did not have to take along a book of poems when she traveled — she had them all in her head, to recall when she wished. She loved poetry, and she loved to memorize poems, which she had done in prodigious amounts from a young age — from Chaucer and Shakespeare to Shelly and Kipling, she knew, loved, and could recite them all.

Red tried to meet and understand the local people wherever she traveled. She tried not to be a tourist, but a traveler, and she tried to blend in wherever she was. She despised the "ugly American" tourists, who seemed to be everywhere, and she always tried to disassociate herself from them.

Red knew Europe quite well, having been many times with her father and other people. She always liked Europe, especially the food on the Continent — the fresh *baguettes* and buttery *croissants* of France, the *schnitzles* and *wursts* of Germany, the pastries and heavy cream of Austria, the wonderful pastas of Italy. Because of the lack of good food, and because of the lousy weather, she generally did not like Great Britain. She never could figure out how the British, being so close to France, never learned to cook very well.

Besides the food, she particularly liked two features of the Continent. One was the way dogs were allowed into stores and restaurants. She thought that was very civilized. Any culture that appreciated their dogs was good in Red's eyes. The second thing she especially liked about Europe was the universal use of "down and duckies" — as her family called those wonderfully soft, thick, and warm down comforters that adorned every bed in every home and in every hotel. Red loved to shop in Europe, and one of the first things her dad bought her there was a big, plump down and ducky to bring home. Believe it or not, even in Florida, with no air-conditioning, she slept under that thing almost every night.

Her brother also traveled to Europe a lot. Duncan was the king of light packers. He would take one pair of pants, one shirt, and all of his old socks and underwear. These he would discard along the way as he used them. This way, he never had to wash out socks and undies, and he got rid of his old ones. Everyone used to laugh at him, teasing him that he left his holey underwear in the best hotels of Europe! What the maids must have thought is hard to say.

Red also spent time in the South Pacific, New Zealand, and Australia, which she enjoyed immensely, as she was an avid scuba diver, but her favorite destination was Latin America. She had traveled extensively in Central America, visiting most of the Mayan ruins, and she really loved the Andes and Incan ruins of South America. As she could speak Spanish, she even traveled there alone sometimes, and I thought her very brave for doing so.

One thing she loved about it was the absence of tourists—especially Americans. As a rule, gringos were not infatuated with South America, and she was glad of it. She loved Peru, with the massive, spectacular Incan ruins perched high in the Andes. She had a very soft spot in her heart for Iquitos, the little backwater town on the Peruvian Amazon, where the jungle was full of her favorite heliconias, bromeliads, monkeys, and parrots.

She took many trips to Brazil, falling under the spell of Rio, "a spectacular city, with mountains coming right down to the sea." Going inland, she visited the largest swamp in the world, the Pantanal, home to the huge and rare hyacinth macaw. This area reminded her of Florida's Everglades, teeming with birdlife and beautiful flora. Then on to the World's largest waterfalls—Iguacu Falls, where, she said, words could not describe the beauty. Brazil remained one of her favorite countries in the world.

On the other side of South America, she traveled to Chile, reaching the very southern tip of Patagonia—Tierra del Fuego—"the land of fire," which was her destination. On subsequent trips to Chile, she even went to Antarctica twice. One time, she flew over to Easter Island.

"Shrimpette," she proclaimed, "everyone who pooh-poohs the over-population problem should go to Easter Island and study what it has to tell us.

As you know, Santayana said, 'those who cannot remember the past are condemned to repeat it.' Everyone should know what happened in the past at Easter Island. Basically, a whole island civilization—the one that produced those fantastic stone heads—procreated itself to death."

"You see, when the population reached the maximum carrying capacity of the island, there was a shortage of life sustaining resources—food and wood. As all the trees were cut down to be used for houses, boats, and fire, the soil began to erode, leaving less arable land for planting, and so even less food could be produced. The people had destroyed their own habitat. Eventually, there was no more wood for boats to be built, so the people could no longer go out to fish, and worse, they could not escape the island."

"There were too many people, not enough food, and no way to escape—can you imagine such a horrific scenario? As a result, intertribal warfare ensued, and in the midst of this, the white man arrived and carried some natives off to the *guano* islands off Peru to be slaves there. Some lived to return, but they brought back with them white man's diseases, most notably smallpox, which finished off what was left of the starving, weakened, native Polynesian population of Easter Island. That was probably a swifter and kinder way to go than starvation, which was what was already happening anyway."

"We need to look at our world as a larger version of Easter Island. As we overpopulate and consume our natural resources, what will happen to us? Already there are wars being fought over finite resources, such as land and fuel, especially oil. Experts predict that by the year 2050, the human population will be ten to twenty billion. How will we produce enough food? With so many people, the wildlife and wildernesses will be mostly gone; will life be worth living?"

20—The End

"Nothing 'Gainst Time's Scythe can make Defense...."
William Shakespeare

When I was older, and I moved away, my life became filled with adult things, and somehow I lost touch with Red. Years later, on returning to our River Road, the first thing I did was to go see Red. I was stunned to find new people living there! Like the river, I expected her to always be there. But instead, strangers were living on Red's property, interlopers who knew nothing about her or her family.

Sadly, the old family homestead was also gone. Although it had been a large home, it had blended into the landscape, hidden by trees and bushes—it had "fit in" with the palm trees and the other old frame River Road homes. In its place was a very large, stucco-cement non-descript house that did not belong. What had been Red's spectacular five acre gardens and citrus groves was now a small housing development. Where there had been one house, now there were five, with asphalt pavement and barren yards, all baking in the Florida sun.

The chickens were all gone—she always maintained she would leave when the chickens could no longer survive.

No trace of her was extant, it was as if her family never existed. Like the Florida panther, they just melted away into the night, away from all the noise, traffic, and development.

I was heartbroken, and felt an emptiness I had never known. I asked everyone who might have known her what had become of her, to no avail. No one seemed to know anything. Some thought she had moved, for she did have a farm somewhere "up north in the hills of the 'deep south'" where she always said she would retreat when things got too crowded in Florida.

"Besides," she had declared years before, "I will have to move from here one day—you know I am next in line to inherit the title of 'Chicken Lady of River Road,' and I'm not so sure I want that title!"

She was increasingly upset over the desecration of our tropical paradise. She swore then that once she left that she would never return, for she could not bear the pain to see things changed for the worse.

Someone thought she may have become ill. In her private way, she had not told a soul of her plans, only cryptically mentioned she was going somewhere more untouched by the heavy hand of man—perhaps echoing Kipling in his poem *On the Road to Mandalay*, a place:

> ...Where the best is like the worst,
> Where there aren't no ten commandments
> And a man can raise a thirst.
> For the temple bells are calling
> And it's there that I would be...

Her parents were by then long dead, and her brother moved away, so I could never solve the mystery. Somehow, I knew that's how Red would've wanted it. She had given my mother two books for me—her favorite copy of the *Bhagavad-Gita*, and a well-worn copy of English poetry. A leather bookmark was at one of Shakespeare's sonnets I had heard her recite from memory—

> ...No longer mourn for me when I am dead,
> Than you shall hear the surly, sullen bell
> Give warning to the world that I am fled
> From this vile world with vilest worms to dwell....

A second bookmark was on John Keats' poem,

> ...To one who has been long in city pent
> Tis very sweet to look into the fair
> And open face of heaven....

Red, her dogs and chickens, and her Indian River paradise were gone forever—but not from my heart or my memory. For it is there that they will reside. I will feel pain for what Red's Florida has become, and rejoice in the happy childhood days spent with them on our beautiful Indian River.

Our River Road, 1932

The good old days, 1950's

21—EPILOGUE

Florida's tragedy continues to this day, and it serves as an ugly reflection of our worldwide *pathos*. Florida's population today is about 17 million, (in 1850, before Flagler built his railroad, it was only about 6,000), and if left unchecked, will be 32 million in the year 2050. Florida is growing by about nine hundred people per day, and over eight hundred acres of land are lost to development *daily*. That translates to over 300,000 new residents a year and 300,000 acres of woods and farmland lost every year. Our wetlands are being drained and filled in at a rate of 13,000 acres per year, and it is estimated that more than half are already gone. These wetlands provide essential habitat for almost all waterfowl—about seventy five percent breed only in wetlands. The wetlands also provide the critical water retention and filtration system for our state.

Florida's new residents (about two-thirds are transplants from other places in the U.S., about eleven percent are foreign immigrants, about one fourth are born here), consume an ADDITIONAL 110,000 gallons of potable water daily, create 94,000 more gallons of sewage and 3,500 more pounds of garbage daily.

The one-hundred-fifty-six mile Indian River Lagoon supports about eighteen percent, or almost two million, of Florida's residents, and is home to more species of plant and animal life, (about 4,300 of them), than any other lagoon system in the United States.

Yet no one will say, "Enough. Florida has had enough growth. We want to maintain some kind of quality of life."

The forces of change, of progress and development with their concomitant destruction of habitat and loss of natural beauty march on ineluctably across our lost tropical paradise.

Red's mom always said, "We need to put up a big fence across the Florida state line to keep people out."

Why won't anyone speak out? As usual, if there's money to be made, nothing else matters. Red explained it to me in simple terms:

"Controlling growth is a very unpopular stance to take with the businessmen and the politicians, and, after all, they are the ones who run the show. Politicians want *more* growth so they have a greater tax base, so they can spend more money on their pet projects, which buy them more votes; businessmen want *more* people so they will make more money. Sadly, it all comes down to the love of the almighty dollar. Quality of life to these people means more money — not more privacy, precious habitat, or beautiful, untouched nature around them. It means more material possessions, not more peace and tranquility. These people have their priorities all wrong, to my way of thinking. This is the sad legacy left to our town by NASA, greedy developers, and 'progressive'-minded businessmen."

As Red maintained, "They are the modern day scalawags and carpetbaggers, come to finish off the job begun by their Yankee relatives one hundred years ago. They have hastened and ensured the end of happy days on the Indian River as we all knew and loved it. Shrimpette," she said one day, "read Dante's *Inferno* and tell me to which circle of Hell the developers will be consigned."

I duly read his masterpiece but confessed I did not know which circle of his *Inferno* would hold the developers.

"I'm not sure, either," Red said, "I believe they will have one all to themselves, there are so many of them, and they are so particularly vile, motivated only by greed. Of course, they will be joined there by the crooked politicians. Hopefully it will be in the hottest circle of Hell."

Her mom regularly proclaimed, "This earth would have been better off if man had never evolved."

And her dad chimed in, "The only good thing that's come out of NASA and growth has been mosquito control, and I'd just as soon live with the 'skeeters as with all the Yankees, growth, and progress."

One does have to wonder why God, in his infinite wisdom, did create humankind. Perhaps we are his most interesting creation, but we are also his most destructive and at times, evil. The pity of it all is we are dragging all of the earth's beautiful flora and innocent fauna down with us in our mad dash to over-procreation and self-destruction.

As Red would say, "I don't care if man drives himself to extinction, in fact that would be great, but to snuff out all the plants and animals too, is criminal.

"Oh well," she shrugged, "no matter what else they do to Florida, there will always be the River. But what it will become is anyone's guess."

I shudder to think what Red and her parents would think of Florida and our world now.

The only thought that gives me comfort is that they could carry away with them an eternal and delectable memory of the salt marshes, the abundant wild life, the pristine beauty of our river; that they could cherish fond memories of a carefree childhood and lifelong friends in a small, friendly town. I am glad that they do not have to see it now, so changed, so permanently scarred and so pitifully altered, a place once so dear to their hearts which is now vanished from this earth forever.

For myself, Red's image will always be etched in my psyche, as she stands with Polly on her back porch calling the chickens to eat, and her voice will forever haunt me, as in a dream. I know I will find her in eternity as soon as I hear the familiar call, plaintive and high-pitched, "Heeeeeere chicky, chick, chick, chick. Here chicky, chick, chick."

About the Author

Mary Eschbach is a sixth generation Floridian and a native of Brevard County.

About the Illustrator

P. G. Willams is a graphic artist who lives in Rockledge, Florida.

An invitation to join...

The Florida Historical Society

Celebrating over 150 years of service to the people of Florida

The Florida Historical Society, founded in 1856, is the only statewide historical society in Florida. The Society is a 501(c)(3) not for profit organization as recognized by the Internal Revenue Service. The primary mission of the Society is to collect, preserve and publish documents and other materials relating to the history of Florida and its peoples.

Membership Benefits Include:
* A complimentary annual subscription to all Society publications: The Florida Historical Quarterly (4 issues) and the Society Report (4 issues).
* A 10% discount on all items in the The Print Shoppe.
* Free admission to the Library and Archives as well as the Saturday Lecture Series.
* Invitations to all events and functions sponsored by the Florida Historical Society.

For Membership Information:
Call: (321) 690 - 1971
Fax: (321) 690 - 4388
e-mail: membership@flahistory.net
website: www.florida-historical-soc.org

www.floridabooks.net/catalog

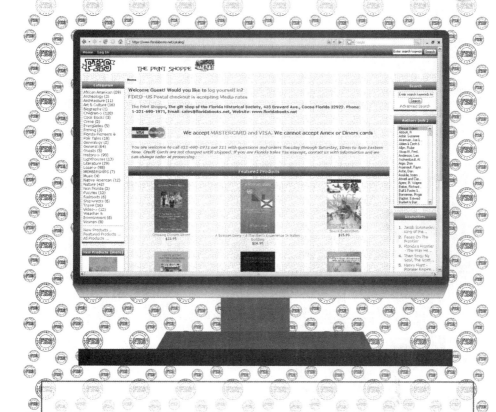

Order Your Florida Books NOW

The Print Shoppe

The book shop of the Florida Historical Society is located at 435 Brevard Ave., Cocoa Florida 32922 and on the internet at www.floridabooks.net

You are welcome to call 321-690-1971 ext 211 with questions and orders Tuesday through Saturday, 10am to 4pm Eastern time. Credit Cards are not charged until shipped. If you are Florida Sales Tax exempt, contact us with information and we can change order at processing.

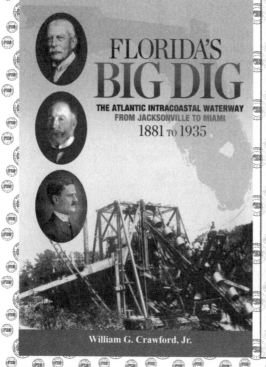